CREATE A WORD IN Taratongue! CONTEST WINNERS

Hey earthkins!

In June 2010, we ran a contest for a word that meant 'Awesome!' in Taratongue (see www.taranauts.com for details). Lots of you sent in lots of words, and they were all winners! But here's the one our jury picked as THE one and it's been used in this adventure of the Taranauts!.

THE GRAND PRIZE WINNING WORD:

MASTASTIC!

AND THE WINNERS:

Dhwani Yagnaraman, 13, Vidya Valley School, Pune

&

Arnav Sinha Roy, 11, Regent International School, Dubai

***

THE WINNERS IN OTHER CATEGORIES!

Most Out-of-the-Box: $O\Sigma$

Read as 'awesome' – the English letter O + the Greek letter Sigma, which stands for 'sum' in Maths.

— Nihaal George, 12, Inventure Academy, Bangalore

Most Original:

1. MANASBLOIN

Use the Sanskrit *manas* for 'mind' in mind-blowing and tweak a bit.

— Srinivasaraghavan, 13, Hari Shree Vidyalam, Chennai

2. EMOSEWA!

'Awesome' backwards.

— Al Azhar, 12, & Arjun Maini, 12, Indus International School, Bangalore

Most Number of Entries:

16! —Tejasvi Rajesh, 12, GD Matric & Higher Secondary School, Coimbatore

62! —The students of Hari Shree Vidyalayam, Chennai

Other Words We Loved:

From earthkins:

* KHOOBACULAR! — Rasika Bharadwaj, 9, Aldenham School, Hertfordshire, UK

* UBERUTTAM! — Anushri Balaji, 12, Emerald Valley Public School, Salem

* MAHASUPER! — Rebecca Anand, 9, St Michael's Academy, Chennai

* JORVELLOUS! — Shrinidhi Prakash, 8, Kingscroft Junior School, Staines, Surrey, UK

* AAHAASOME! — Siddharth Chokkalingam, 13, Hari Shree Vidyalam, Chennai

* WAHBULOUS! — Ramya Jaishankar, 13, Still Middle School, Naperville, Illinois, USA

* AWESEMMA! — Sruthi Rajmohan, 11, Hari Shree Vidyalam, Chennai

* FANTADIA! — Nikita Sagar, 9, Headstart Montessori, Bangalore

From older earthkos:

* ZABAROOVY! — Monica Pillai, mental age 12, Bangalore

* FABKHOO! — Priti Doshi, Bangalore

* ZABARCOOL — Shachii Manik, Mumbai

We hope you enjoy our mastastic third adventure!

TARANAUTS ZARPA, ZVALA, AND TUFAN

* 'MASTASTIC' WINNERS GET BOOKS WORTH RS 1500 + TARANAUTS SUPERSTUFF FROM HACHETTE INDIA

* ALL WINNERS GET A GIFT HAMPER FROM HACHETTE INDIA (TARANAUTS POSTER + MOUSEPAD + BADGES)

* HARI SHREE VIDYALAYAM, CHENNAI, GETS A BOOK HAMPER FOR THE LIBRARY + MOUSEPADS FROM HACHETTE INDIA

* ALL PARTICIPANTS GET SURPRIZES!

taranauts

THE SECRET OF THE
SPARKL
AMETHYSTS

CHASE THE STARS AT
www.taranauts.com

Roopa Pai suspects she has alien blood, for two reasons. One, she loved history in school. And two, although an adult, she mostly reads children's books.

Roopa has won a Children's Book Trust award for science writing. Among her published works are a four-book science series, *Sister Sister* (Pratham Books), and two girl-power books, *Kaliyuga Sita* and *Mechanic Mumtaz* (UNICEF).

When she is not dreaming up plots for her stories, she goes on long solo bicycle rides, and takes children on history and nature walks in Bangalore. You can find her at *www.roopapai.in*.

taranauts
BOOK THREE

THE SECRET OF THE
SPARKL
AMETHYSTS

Roopa Pai

Illustrated by Priya Kuriyan

First published in 2010 by Hachette India
An Hachette UK company

www.hachetteindia.com

10 9 8 7 6 5 4 3 2 1

ISBN: 978-93-80143-53-8

Hachette India
612/614 (6th Floor), Time Tower
MG Road, Sector 28, Gurgaon 122001, India

Typeset in Perpetua 13.5/16 by
Eleven Arts, New Delhi

Printed in India by
Manipal Press Ltd, Manipal

For Mon My Nit,
mastastic team, good sports,
always game

TAF

Magmacup

MegaStage

Zum Skar

KAY
LAA

Magmalift

Glo

Dazl

Syntilla

Lustr

Shaap Azur

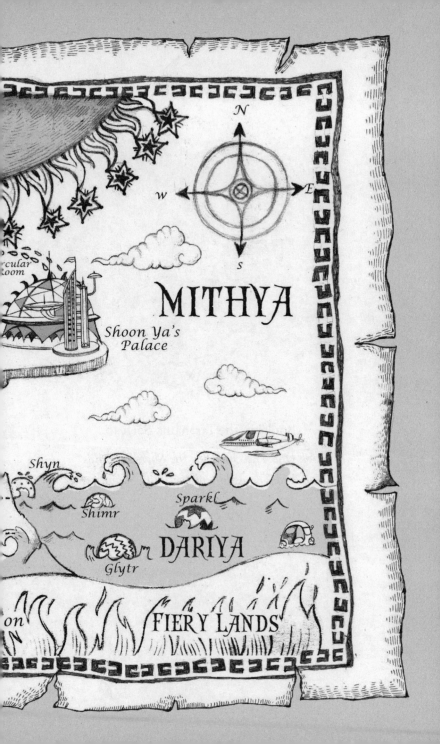

Books in the Taranauts Series

Taranauts
The Trail of the Tale

Eight octons after the wise, brave Shoon Ya became Emperaza, Mithya was celebrating with the grandest Octoversary ever. For the first time, the 32 stars of Tara—the glorious supersun with the cool rainbow coloured light—had come down to dance at the celebrations. But their show was rudely interrupted by Shoon Ya's evil twin, Shaap Azur, who broke out of his prison below the heaving seabed of Dariya and captured all 32 stars in the Silver Spinternet, plunging Mithya into darkness.

The stars could be rescued, but only if the 32 riddles Shaap Azur had hidden on the eight worlds were solved within an octet. Enter sweet-faced Zvala, child of Fire, athletic Zarpa, child of the SuperSerpent Shay Sha, and animal magnet Tufan, child of the Wind—three gifted mithyakins chosen by the Emperaza several octons ago to save Mithya from the Great Crisis.

Under the watchful eye of Shuk Tee, the Emperaza's most trusted advisor, and the guidance of three expert Achmentors—hypnotic Achalmun, who trains their minds, scatterbrained Dummaraz, who strengthens their values, and full-of-fun Twon d'Ung, who fine-tunes their bodies—the Taranauts begin to blossom into brave, strong, responsible heroes.

For their first challenge, the Taranauts travelled to Zvala's home world of Shyn with their new friend Makky, a makara with an amazing sense of smell. After many exciting adventures that tested their fledgling powers to the hilt, they cracked the hidden riddles and rescued the four Tarasuns of Shyn—the Emeralds.

An octoll later, the Taranauts were off again, this time to the brain-scrambling Mayazaal in Lustr, Tufan's home world, where they met the mysterious Zubreymunyun. Despite Zub's disconcerting habit of disappearing from the scene without explanation, he helped the Taranauts overcome several dangers, including flesh-eating flowers, weeping trees and hostile minimits, before they eventually rescued the four stars of Lustr—the Sapphires.

If the rescue of the Emeralds drove Shaap Azur to a fury, the sight of the freed Sapphires in Mithya's sky has him vowing revenge. With his six able Ograzurs and an army of Demazurs and Downsiders behind him, he is a formidable enemy, more than a match for three mithyakins, gifted or otherwise. Or is he? Now read on . . .

Mithyology

Mithya A whole different universe, with eight worlds—Dazl, Glo, Shyn, Shimr, Lustr, Sparkl, Syntilla, Glytr—that bob around in the endless sea of **Dariya**, around the bad-tempered volcano **Kay Laas**. On top of Kay Laas, in the Land of Eternal Taralite, lives ShoonYa, the Emperaza of Mithya.

Tara The rainbow-coloured supersun of Mithya. Tara has 32 stars in eight iridescent colours—the Emeralds, the Sapphires, the Amethysts, the Rubies, the Citrines, the Silvers, the Turquoises, and the Corals.

Tarasuns The 32 stars that make up Tara.

Taraday A day on Mithya. It is 48 dings long.

Taralite From 1 o'ding to 32 o'ding, the Upsides of the eight worlds, where most mithyakos live, stay out of the water and enjoy the cool colourful light of the Tarasuns. This part of the Taraday is called Taralite.

Fliptime At 32 o'ding, all the worlds flip over into Dariya. The moment when this happens is called Fliptime.

Taranite From Fliptime until 48 o'ding, the Upsides are turned away from Tara and into Dariya. During this time, they are in darkness, their buildings and vehicles and forests protected with force-fields called **Dar-Proofs** which prevent water from seeping in.

Downsides The halves of each world that stay in darkness, inside Dariya, for 32 dings each Taraday. These are scary, unexplored places, populated by creatures of the darkness and not-so-nice mithyakos.

Xad Yuntra The secret hideout of Shaap Azur, Emperaza Shoon Ya's evil twin.

Magmalift A magma-powered elevator inside Kay Laas in which mithyakos can zoom up to the Land of Eternal Taralite.

Aquauto An amphibious cab with the ability to travel both on water and on land.

Aqualimo A much fancier aquauto used by VIMs (Very Important Mithyakos) to get around.

Cabamba Another kind of cab—but this one travels only on land.

Magnarail A superfast train.

For more words in Taratongue, see *Taranauts Book One: The Quest for the Shyn Emeralds.*

one

Tufan opened his closet at Zum Skar and spent five whole dinglings in glorious indecision—which of the eight autographed special-edition Lustr Blasters tees hanging there should he wear to class today?

His mind flew back to the octite after the Taranauts had rescued the Lustr Sapphires, when the coolest blast metal band in the universe had invited him—yes, *him*, Tufan, the weird mithyakin from Lustr!—to jam with them on stage. It had been completely mastastic! He remembered how the Lustrkos had screamed his name, pressed themselves against the stage, stretched their hands out for him to shake, crowded around . . .

'Mithya to Tufan! Mithya to Tufan! Do you read, Taranaut Tufan?'

Tufan jumped. 'Loud and clear!' he snapped, leaping into the closet and pulling the door shut behind him.

A dingling later, he stuck his face around the door and scowled at Zvala and Zarpa. Then his jaw dropped.

'Ex-*cuse* me,' he said testily. 'Where in Kay Laas did you two get those yuckthoo-pink, glittery LB tees from, may I ask? I bet they were designed by some sillykoof who doesn't know a blast guitarele from a meenmaach's tail!' His eyes narrowed. 'You guys are completely ruining the LBs' reputation—the LBs are *not*, repeat *not*, Dana Suntana! Plus, it's a copyright violation to have your own tees designed . . .' He glared accusingly at Zvala.

'Well, of all the . . .' Zvala burst out angrily, crunching her already-flaming red hands into indignant fists. 'I will have you know that the LBs themselves got these tees designed for us, *extra*-special editions, as a personal gift for rescuing the Sapphires . . .'

'Exactly!' said Zarpa, 'And, for your *kind* information, it was Zvala who insisted we wear them today because she thought it would make you happy.'

The face around the door relented a little, but grudgingly. '*We-ell*, if they gave them to you themselves, I guess . . .'

'Yes, they did!' said Zvala, still annoyed. 'In fact, it was that cute drummer guy who handed them over . . .'

Tufan winced in real pain. The LBs were cool, mastastic, genius, epic, killer—but *cute*? He tossed desperately about for ways to change the subject.

'By the way,' he snapped, 'who gave you the permission to walk into my room without knocking?'

Zvala sighed. 'We knocked and knocked,' she held up her hands mournfully, her fingers all folded inwards at the second joint, 'until our fingers fell off.' On cue, Zarpa held up her own 'half-fingers', her mouth pulled into an inverted U.

Tufan tried hard to resist, then gave up the fight. The face split into a huge grin. 'Uffpah! You guys are such absolute . . . *loontoons*!'

The girls laughed.

'See you at breakfast in two,' said Zarpa, the most responsible of the three, pointing to her dingdial. 'Or you starve until lunchtime.'

'And puh-*leese*,' begged Zvala, 'go easy on the Max . . .'

'I read! I read!' barked the face. 'Now go!'

Noisily slurping up the last few drops of her powertein-packed aamberry flipfloat, Zvala raced out of the dining hall at Zum Skar and towards the circular tower room at the palace. She took the stairs three at a time, bursting in just one dingling before the door opened again.

'All ready for your first session this morning?' Resplendent in scarlet astersilk, Shuk Tee swept regally into the tower room.

'Oh, yes, Ms Shuk Tee,' panted Zvala, as the

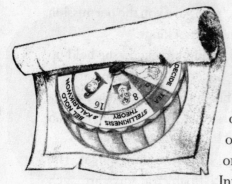

Taranauts shot to their feet, their backs ramrod straight. For some reason, thought Zvala—maybe because she rarely smiled, or because she was second only to Emperaza Shoon Ya, or because she was the Most Intelligent Being in Mithya, or because she was so . . . um . . . *tall*—Shuk Tee's mere presence in a room was awe-inspiring.

'Here are your dingplans for the octoll,' said Shuk Tee, handing out scrolls of palmyra. 'Your first session today is with Achmentor Achalmun.'

Tufan's face lit up—he adored the dour, enigmatic Achmentor, even if he found his brain-bending sessions a little difficult to cope with. Zvala groaned inwardly—Achalmun and his mind-reading eyes disturbed her intensely, for reasons she could not explain.

She scanned the lesson list quickly and felt a sudden rush of excitement—whatever she felt about Achalmun, there was certainly some great stuff to look forward to at his sessions—apart from the regular puzzles, ciphers and optical illusions, there was also *Introduction* to *Stellikinesis*—the science of moving objects with your willpower, and *Hovitation 101*—the art of floating in mid-air for several dinglings at a time.

Next to Zvala, Zarpa was also examining her dingplan, trying to calculate just how many dings per octite the

Taranauts were going to work with their favourite Achmentor, the young, fun Twon d'Ung. Under her watchful, appreciative eye, Zarpa got to perfect the kind of stuff she loved—leaping and somersaulting through the air in Kalarikwon, twisting and bending and flexing every single muscle doing Yogaichi, and racing across the sports field playing one game or another. Her pulse raced as she saw the games schedule—this time they were going to be playing Bel Nolo, which meant they would have to learn to ride ashvequins first!

'Three dings with Twon d'Ung,' Zarpa mouthed triumphantly to her teammates. Shuk Tee sipped her morning cup of brunesca.

'Yayyy!' Zvala gave her a thumbs-up. She didn't particularly enjoy the punishing stretches and crunches of the fitness sessions, and the thought of galloping around on a dangerously fast ashvequin didn't exactly fill her with joy, but there were always laughs and treats and chatter when Twon d'Ung was around. Plus, all that sweating in the games field seemed to have done wonders for her normally pale, dull skin—even Ma had noticed. 'And three with Dummaraz!'

It was Tufan's turn to grin. Three dings with absent-minded Achmentor Dummaraz, who taught them how to deal with problems of right and wrong, meant three dings of freedom to do whatever they liked. Particularly when Dummaraz got so involved with one of his problems that he spent the rest of the session arguing with himself!

Burrrr! Burrrr! On Shuk Tee's desk, her summoner

began to vibrate. 'It's the Emperaza calling,' said ShukTee, dismissing them with a wave of her hand. 'Go to your lessons now.'

Bowing slightly, the Taranauts made their way silently out of the tower room.

'Last one down the stairs is a soggy samchori!' cried Tufan, jumping on to the winding banister the moment the massive door had shut behind them.

'See you at the bottom, loser!' Zarpa rose to the challenge instantly, zipping down the stairs in her Obverse nanos.

'Hey! No fair!' wailed Zvala, racing down as fast as she could in her delicate pink-and-silver sandals.

KRR-RRRASH!

'Serves Tufan right!' thought Zvala gleefully to herself as she leaned over the banister to check the damage. Then she choked back a giggle. It was better than she could have hoped. At the bottom of the stairs, next to a very embarrassed Tufan, sprawled a furious Achmentor Achalmun!

Two

Somewhere on the Downside, standing at the window of the throne room in his shining blue-black crystal citadel, a tall, powerfully-built mithyaka stared moodily out at the rocky landscape. Around his waist, he wore a length of worn but clean homespun. His dark hair was cropped close to his skull. The strong, angular face was clean-shaven, and the smooth brown skin shone with good health.

'You wished to see me?'

Shaap Azur whirled from the window. Ograzur Vak, who had just come in, drew in his breath in a sharp gasp. When Shaap Azur, master of illusion, assumed his normal form, the resemblance to his twin brother, Emperaza Shoon Ya, was striking. The only feature that was markedly different were the eyes—Shoon Ya's wide open, honest, trusting and friendly, Shaap Azur's small and mean, perennially filled with anger, hate and bitterness. Vak had known both the twins since they were little mithyakins, and had taught them most of what they knew.

'Achmentor, come in. Sit down.' Shaap Azur took his place on his polished black tantrite throne and waved Vak into a low seat. 'This is a council of war. I have asked the other Ograzurs to come in as well, in a little while. But I wanted to talk to you first.'

Vak nodded, waiting.

'Eight Tarasuns have been freed already, Achmentor— *eight*! The whole of Mithya—all those supercilious Upsiders—are laughing up their sleeves at us. My own people—the minimits, the Rapacious Voracious flower spirits—are beginning to question my authority! Shoon Ya's brats are becoming heroes, just like him. It makes my blood boil!'

He paused, his eyes narrowing. 'Shoon Ya has not done right by me, Achmentor. Mithya should have been mine, by right. I was always the brighter student, was I not? The smarter one, second only to Shuk Tee? Among the best at mind control? And always, always, one of the champions at the Mithyolympics?'

Vak nodded at his favourite student. 'Yes, you were, no doubt about that,' he said gently. 'But you are wrong when you say Shoon Ya has not done right by you. We all know that he was chosen by the elders of the Mithyacouncil to become Emperaza eight octons ago, fair and square. You remember that, don't you?'

How could he *not*? Shaap Azur's face clouded over at the memory of that Taralite-drenched evening when the announcement had been made at Megastage. He had had a great morning at the Bel Nolo Exhibition Match, thundering across the field on his favourite wilderwolf, slamming more than half the discs home and beating Shoon Ya's team to pulp, while a mazillion mithyakos cheered and shouted his name. Later, at the lavish lunch party for Emperaza candidates, he had chatted and laughed with his brother and Shuk Tee, confident that, a few dings later, he would be stepping up to the crystal throne in the Land of Nevernite.

And then . . .

Shaap Azur shook the memory away angrily, surprised that it still had the power to hurt so much. 'Even so, Achmentor,' he hissed through clenched teeth, 'Shoon Ya could have intervened, had his say, chosen me to rule Mithya side by side with him. His own twin brother! Instead, he banished me to the Fiery Lands, imprisoned me, like I was some kind of monster . . .'

'Shaap, Shaap, don't twist the facts,' Vak's voice had an edge to it. 'ShoonYa offered you the position of Dewanaza of the Downside, declared to all of Mithya that his brilliant brother was the only one he could trust to keep the rebellious Downsiders under control. You accepted—with rather bad grace, I might add—but once you took charge at XadYantra, you began plotting against the Emperaza—your own brother. You incited the Downsiders to mischief against the Upsiders, and all hell broke loose. You lost the love of the mithyakos, Shaap, and ShoonYa had no choice but to banish you to the Fiery Lands . . .'

Shaap Azur turned furiously upon his old teacher. 'So now *you* are on his side as well, Achmentor!' he fumed. 'Why don't you go and join him, then, like loyal little yes-sir-no-sir ShukTee? If I had been chosen Emperaza, she would have ruled with me as my equal, which is only what she deserves. But she preferred to *serve* instead, as an underling, second-best to the Most Glorious ShoonYa.' He shook his head in bewilderment. '*Why* would anyone do that?'

Vak stood up, his face sad. 'I am not abandoning you just yet, Shaap. I still live in hope that my brightest one will do his duty by Mithya. Abandon this vile scheme immediately, free the Tarasuns—it is not too late . . . .'

Shaap Azur looked at his teacher as if he thought he was mad. 'I *cannot* and *will* not ever do that,' he raged. 'Don't you see? If I do that, that's the end—no mithyaka, not even a mithayakin, will ever respect me again. And . . .'

Someone was knocking at the door. Shaap Azur quickly composed himself. 'Come in!'

The other Ograzurs shuffled in—brash young Dusht, the vicious siblings Raaksh and Shurpa, cruel Hidim Bi, and dreamy Paapi. They kept their eyes lowered, afraid to face their Master's fury. They had failed him again, and they knew this meeting would not be pleasant.

'So,' said Shaap Azur, his voice dripping sarcasm, 'my capable, hand-picked, *star* team of lieutenants from across Mithya—what have you got to say for yourself?'

The Ograzurs kept their eyes on the floor.

'I WANT ANSWERS!' roared Shaap Azur, slamming his fist down on the throne arm. The Ograzurs flinched as if they had been whipped. 'And ideas! *Ideas*, anyone? ANYONE?'

Dusht raised his head. 'I have one,' he said, his voice even. 'It will be slow, and dangerous, but if it works, very deadly . . .'

'Out with it, Dusht! Tough times call for tough measures.'

'What we need,' Dusht looked straight at his master, 'is a mole, a traitor on the other side . . .'

· RAAKSH ·

· PAAPI ·

· SHURPA ·

· HIDIM BI ·

· DUSHT ·

A brief spark of interest lit up Shaap Azur's face.

Dusht saw it, and moved quickly. 'With your permission, I will begin making enquiries. Very discreetly, of course.'

'Master,' began Vak, who was always careful to address Shaap Azur thus when there were others present, 'it isn't too late to seek an audience with the Emperaza, to start a dialogue . . .'

The Ograzurs turned on Vak, their eyes blazing. 'And get sent back to the Fiery Lands?' screeched Hidim Bi. 'Are you out of your mind, you crazy old mithyaka?'

'Shut your foul mouth, Hidim Bi,' roared Shaap Azur, but he would not meet Vak's eyes. 'No one speaks to Ograzur Vak that way, at least not in my presence. Council dismissed! We meet again in two octites. Dusht, stay behind—there are matters I need to discuss with you.'

Vak hung back from the others, trying to get Shaap Azur's attention, but the erstwhile Dewanaza of the Downside had returned to his place by the window. Shaking his head worriedly, Vak turned and left the room.

Three

'Who's the team with the big, big dream?
We a-a-are, we are!
We're the best, we're off on a quest,
We'll ra-a-aise the bar!
We'll crack each clue and we'll rescue
Each glo-o-owing star!'

With a final, session-ending whoop, the Taranauts gathered around Twon d'Ung, breathless.

'I can't decide which one is more fun—' panted Tufan, 'dying of exhaustion each octite we spend at Zum Skar, or nearly getting killed by shrinking wells and weeping trees when we are out on our rescue missions.'

The others laughed. 'And the octite isn't even over yet!' groaned Zvala. 'There's still some aaaa . . . uuuu . . . . mmmming to be done before we turn in.'

'Dinner is in less than a ding,' cautioned Twon d'Ung. 'So you'd better be on your way quickly if you want to catch a shower before that.'

'I'm off!' cried Tufan, jumping up immediately. The girls rolled their eyes—Tufan and his mazillion showers a day! 'It's not the *shower*, dum-dums. I haven't seen Makky since I got back here and this is the only chance I'll have today. Coming?'

'You bet!' Zvala and Zarpa scrambled to their feet. 'Bye, Ms Twon d'Ung! See you tomorrow!'

They sprinted off towards the royal stables, Tufan pausing only to pick up his bright-eyed gileli Squik and his stripy kipchali Chik-Chik from the Animal Care Centre on the way. The little creatures leapt into his palms with happy squeaks, then headed straight for their usual places in his pockets where they knew their favourite zamunberries would be waiting.

'He can smell us coming already!' marvelled Zarpa, when they were still a long way off, grinning at the loud excited grunts coming from the direction of the stables. 'Poor old chap—he has really missed us!'

'Almost there, boy!' called Zvala, as the three of them put on an extra burst of speed towards their beloved Makky.

'Full focus!' growled Achmentor Achalmun. 'Attempt anew!'

It was the fourth octite after the Taranauts had returned to Zum Skar, and training had settled into a regular routine. Tufan had been having a rough time as usual at Achalmun's sessions, but he never stopped trying to impress the humourless Achmentor. Today, in their first-ever Stellikinesis lesson, Tufan was determined to make an impression.

Clenching his fists and staring hard at the glowing disc at the centre of the table, he willed it to slide towards him. For the mazillionth time, the disc lay absolutely still. Achalmun shook his head in disgust. Tufan's shoulders slumped, defeated.

At the next table, Zarpa was not having much better luck. She closed her eyes, repeated the Chant of Deep Stillness in her head, took a deep breath, and focused hard. The disc obstinately refused to move. 'Perpetual practice,' advised Achalmun, his tone almost paternal. Zarpa nodded, grateful that he never seemed to get mad at her. She looked over to see how Zvala was doing.

Zvala was staring fixedly at her disc, but she could feel her concentration begin to flag. Her razor-sharp brain had been very useful to the Taranauts in cracking puzzles and solving riddles, but her attention span had always been limited. Now, at the fag end of Achalmun's session, after 'full focusing' for almost three dings, she had had enough. 'I can't do it,' she sighed. 'It's too hard.'

Anger blazed in Achalmun's face, and the constantly changing indigo-gold tattoo on his smooth pate went absolutely still. 'Wasted gifts,' he fumed. 'Indolent ingrate!'

Zvala frowned. She hated it when people used words she did not understand. From the way Achalmun said them, though, she was quite certain they were not complimentary. She felt anger course through her. How dare he! She would show him the stuff she was made of!

She forced herself to calm down, then focused once again on the disc. For a dingling or two, nothing happened, and then the disc shuddered. Zvala clenched her teeth and stared at the disc, her eyes boring a hole through it. The disc shuddered again, and then, miraculously, moved a fraction of a centinch towards her!

Zvala was so surprised she forgot to be angry. 'Achmentor!' she whispered, her eyes shining with wonder. 'I did it!'

'Lucky fluke,' barked Achalmun, glaring at her. 'Practise harder.' He stared at the three glowing discs. They sped across the tables towards him, then flew straight into his wide sleeves. 'Class dismissed!' Turning on his heel, he strode from the room.

Zvala felt hot, hurt tears prick the back of her eyes. Why could she never seem to do anything that pleased Achalmun? Quickly, before those tears spilled out embarrassingly, she stuffed her things into her backsack and fled to the washroom.

Achmentor Dummaraz bustled into the classroom muttering to himself, his hair and glasses askew, his wide pyjamas flapping around his legs. 'Sit down, sit down, my mithyakins,' he said, barely touching their bowed heads. 'Welcome back. Great job with the Sapphires, by the way.'

'Today's topic,' he rifled hastily through the huge sheaf of papers he was carrying, sending most of them sliding off the table to the ground, 'is about choices. Good choices and bad choices. Are bad people good people who made bad choices? Or are good people bad people who made good choices? Do good people make good choices because they are bad?'

He stopped and shook his head so vigorously that it swivelled around to the back before it came once again to face them. 'Scratch that. I meant "Do good people make bad people because they are choices?" He stopped again, thoroughly confused.

The Taranauts giggled. Tufan winked at the girls.

'Tell us, Achmentor,' he said, putting on his most innocent face. 'Is Shaap Azur a good person who made bad choices because he didn't know how to make good

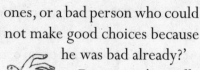

ones, or a bad person who could not make good choices because he was bad already?'

Dummaraz's usually slack, distracted face snapped suddenly to tense attention. He searched Tufan's face intently. 'Are you being sassy with me, mithyakin?' he demanded.

'Oh, no, sir!' lied Tufan, taken aback by the sudden change in his teacher.

'Well, then,' said Dummaraz, although he did not look completely convinced. 'If you really want my opinion, Shaap Azur always had, and continues to have, the potential for greatness. I was part of the junior staff at Zum Skar when he was a student here, and I remember him well. Bright as a button he was, and talented, too—President of the Debating Society three octons running . . .'

He turned to the scribescreen behind him and began to write furiously on it. 'You know, I never missed a Bel Nolo game that he was playing in—what a sportsman!' He paused. 'Quite a hero, really, our Shaap Azur . . . I've often wondered what would have happened if he had become Emperaza—he might have been one of our best . . .'

'Sir!' interrupted Zarpa, looking aghast. 'Do you really mean that? That you think Shaap Azur would have made a good Emperaza?'

Dummaraz's shoulders tensed ever so slightly. When he turned around, he looked his usual preoccupied self again. 'Umm . . . were we talking about the Emperaza?' he wheezed, gathering up his fallen papers clumsily, dropping his scratchscribes all over the floor as he did so. 'Weren't we talking about choices?" He chuckled suddenly. "Ahh, I see now—you are trying to *distract* me, aren't you?" His eyes twinkled. "Nice try, mithyakin, but I'm too old an Achmentor to fall for your tricks."

The Taranauts sneaked a quick look at each other. Had Achmentor Dummaraz really forgotten what they were talking about, or was it all an act put on for their benefit?

Four

Zarpa peeked through the shimmery curtains on MegaStage at the crowds of cheering mithyakos. She had thought she would get used to this, that there would be no titliflies in her stomach when they had to choose the world that they would travel to this time, but she had been wrong. Every single mithyaka out there seemed so confident that the Taranauts would succeed once again—but *could* they? Who knew what horrible obstacles Shaap Azur was planning to put in their way? What if they were not able to crack a riddle or two? How would they cope if their superskills failed them at a crucial time?

'This is sooooo exciting!' squealed Zvala, sticking her face next to Zarpa's. Cool black kankohl lined her eyes, her lips glowed with nectanger balm, and her hair twinkled and sparkled like it had stars in it.

Tufan squeezed in beside her. 'Woo-hoo!' he exulted. 'Look at the crowds—the Taranauts are a sell-out act!'

Zarpa sighed—the others obviously did not share her concerns in the least.

'Uffpah, go *away* before I die of Maxphyxiation!' grumbled Zvala, tossing her hair into Tufan's face.

'Oh, *do*!' snapped Tufan, shading his eyes and pushing her away. 'We'll be quits then! You die of Maxphyxiation, I get blinded by your headlights!'

Zvala looked puzzled for a moment, then she began to chortle. 'They are not *head*lights, you sillykoof, they are glolights! But tell me, do they look good? And do you want some in your hair?' Tufan fled. Zvala raced after him, holding out her tube of glolight gel like a dangerous weapon.

'Sssstop it, you two!' yelled Zarpa, exasperated. 'We go onstage in ten dinglingsss!'

Zvala shot her friend a concerned look. Zarpa's lisp only showed up when she was really stressed. 'Relax, Zarpa! This time, the whole Megastage thing is no big deal—we've already decided which world we're going to next.'

'You should be happy, Zarpa!' added Tufan. 'You are going *home*!'

Zarpa looked even more miserable. Maybe that was what was making her so grouchy and anxious—the fear that she would let Mama and Papa and the rest of the Sparklkos down by failing to save the Amethysts.

There was a flourish of crescent horns and conch shells. The Taranauts fled into the wings as the curtains parted and Emperaza Shoon Ya rode majestically onto Megastage on his snarling shardula. Deafening cheers and applause filled the air.

'Good people of Mithya,' boomed the Emperaza, turning his face up to the faint azure-emerald Taralite. 'Do the Sapphires not add a splendid touch to the day?'

The crowd cheered. Then the chanting began. 'Taranauts! Tara-NAUTS!' Shoon Ya smiled.

Shuk Tee stepped forward, her hand raised for silence. 'Before the Taranauts come on, there are a few announcements . . .'

The rest of her sentence was drowned out—the crowd wanted nothing but their heroes. 'Tara-NAUTS! Tara-NAUTS!'

Shuk Tee frowned, raising her hand once again. 'But this is important! There is a certain protocol . . .'

'Tara-NAUTS! Tara-NAUTS!'

Shoon Ya raised an imperious hand. Shuk Tee looked pleased—the mithyakos may not always listen to her, but they would certainly do as their beloved Emperaza commanded.

'You shall have your wish, mithyakos!' declared Shoon Ya. 'Get on stage, Taranauts!'

'But . . . Emperaza!' protested Shuk Tee, her eyes flashing with anger, but it was too late. The band had struck up a merry tune, and the Taranauts were already striding in from the wings to ear-splitting cheers. Her mouth set in a grim line, Shuk Tee took her place next to Shoon Ya as the map of Mithya came up on the giant screen.

When the cheering had died down a little, Shuk Tee clicked on the Riddles icon. The northern and southern worlds of Shyn and Lustr lit up immediately. But unlike the previous two times, the other worlds remained dark and untagged. The Taranauts exchanged quick glances—what did it mean?

'So, Taranauts,' broke in Shoon Ya, 'which world shall it be this time?'

Zarpa cleared her throat nervously, straightened her shoulders, and looked him in the eye. 'We've chosen Sssparkl, Emperaza,' she said.

BOOM! A flash of brilliant light exploded on screen, blinding the Taranauts. When they could focus again, they saw that the picture on the screen had changed a little—each world was now tagged, but differently from before. This time, the words held a deeper menace.

'Glytr—Terror Trail,' stuttered Zvala, in the sudden hush that had fallen over the crowd. 'Syntilla—Pain & Peril, Glo—Hostage Horror, Dazl—Deadly Danger, Shimr—Manic Monsters . . .' Then she stopped, her eyes round with fright. Zarpa and Tufan gulped. They were all staring at Sparkl. On the world they had chosen for their next mission was stamped just one terrifying word—ENDGAME!

'Oh, Pappy, Zarpy's sssso glad you are here!' Zarpa leaped into her dad's arms as he stepped out of the Magmalift.

'Uffpah!' groaned Zarpa's dad in mock irritation, as she climbed nimbly onto his shoulders and threw her arms tight around his head. 'Do you *have* to be a little monkapi, Zarpa? What will your friends think?'

'Oh, I'm sorry, guys!' Zarpa stood up on her dad's shoulders and jumped to the ground, turning a perfect somersault on the way. 'Meet my dad!' she sang, skipping over to Zvala and Tufan. 'And Papa, meet my mastastic pals.' Then she was off again, turning cartwheels around the three of them. 'Pappy!' she called, zigzagging away. 'Come watch Zarpy do Kalarikwon!'

'Coming, puchkin!' Zarpa's dad smiled apologetically at Zvala and Tufan, and raced after her.

Zvala stared. Whatever had happened to the Zarpa she knew? For one thing, she had suddenly lost her lisp again, which was good—it meant she was ready to take charge of the mission in her cool-headed, responsible way. But this dancing, singing little mithyatot did not inspire any confidence at all. She shot a quick look at Tufan—he looked equally baffled. Their eyes met and the same question passed between them—did Zarpa just call herself *Zarpy*? And her dad *Pappy*?

Tufan snorted. Zvala hooted. Collapsing to the ground,

they laughed until the tears ran down their cheeks.

'And may I enquire into the cause of all this merriment?'

Tufan and Zvala shot to their feet, trying to stifle their giggles. 'Oh, hello, Ms Shuk Tee,' said Tufan, wiping his eyes. 'It's nothing—just a private joke.'

Shuk Tee's mouth curled up slightly at the edges. ' 'Here's Makky—he's all set.' The makara made small, happy sounds as Tufan pulled its ears affectionately. Shuk Tee looked around her. 'The question is,' she said slowly, 'are *you*?'

'Oh yes, Ms Shuk Tee,' said Zvala quickly. 'Zarpy is . . .' Tufan buried his face in Makky's side, his shoulders shaking. 'I mean . . . Zarpa . . . is right here. She was just showing her dad around. Let me go and find them . . .' She fled.

Two dinglings later, she was back, Zarpa and her dad in tow. In Shuk Tee's presence, Zarpa turned into her sensible old self again. 'We've gone over the checklist several times, Ms Shuk Tee,' she said, pointing to their backsacks. 'But . . . do we have any status updates at all? On what . . . um . . . *Endgame* might mean? We have no idea where to start looking once we get to Sparkl.'

'Not yet, I'm afraid,' said Ms Shuk Tee. 'But Shaap Azur is not one to leave things half done. He loves attention,' her mouth twisted in disdain, 'and he will want Mithya to see just how smart he has been about creating and hiding the riddles. I have a feeling the Marani will have received a message of some sort by the time you reach Sparkl.'

'All right, then, Ms Shuk Tee. Wish us luck!'

'Go well, Taranauts.' She touched their bowed heads quickly. 'And the aqualimo?'

'All in place, Ms Shuk Tee,' Zarpa's dad assured her. 'As the official representative of the government of Sparkl, I shall see that the Taranauts lack for nothing.'

Shuk Tee nodded. Gathering up their backsacks and hurrying Makky along, the three Taranauts raced to the Magmalift.

Five

Zarpa stopped pacing the floor for a dingling. 'Your Starness,' she asked for the mazillionth time, 'are you quite, *quite* certain no Sparklkos have called in yet?'

'I'm sure they have,' replied the Marani, 'but all their leads must have turned out to be duds. If not, one of my officers would have alerted us instantly.'

Sixteen dings had passed since the Taranauts had arrived at the Marani's official residence on Sparkl. Fliptime was less than a ding away, but they were still completely in the dark about what Endgame meant, or where they should start. They had pored in vain over their maps, speculated endlessly with the Sparklographers, and had had several fruitless conversations with Shuk Tee and their achmentors before the communications systems had shut down.

In the last eight dings, responding to a request from the Marani, trizillions of Sparklkos had been out scouring their neighbourhoods for anything unusual or suspicious, something that could serve as a starting point for the Taranauts' mission. But so far, the Marani's summoner had stayed silent.

Zarpa began pacing the floor again, cracking her knuckles nervously. She wanted to be out there and *doing* something to rescue the Amethysts. If they didn't get started soon, the octoll would run out, and then, and then . . . A red mist swam before her eyes. It was all that wicked Shaap Azur's fault. If she ever got to meet him face to face, she would . . .

She stomped hard on the ground and shook her fists. 'What'sss the matter, Shaap Azur?' she taunted. 'Sssscared your riddles are too easy for us? Huh? Huh?'

A horrified hush fell over the room. Zvala and Tufan glanced fearfully out of the windows and instinctively went back-to-back in a defensive Kalarikwon position, bracing themselves for Shaap Azur's wrath. But Zarpa wasn't done yet.

'Shaap Azur'sss a ssscaredy-cat!' she sang fearlessly. 'Cowardy cowardy crepohhh-sssaaa!'

KRR-RRASHH!

With a bone-rattling crash, all the windows of the

room shattered. Through the empty frames came a great flock of giant kakrows, glossy black wings flapping furiously, beady eyes darting hither and thither, sharp cruel beaks and curved talons at the ready. Cawing in ear-splitting cacophony, they perched on the arcalamps, folded them in their wings, and turned everything black as pitch. Everyone screamed and dropped to the floor, their hands covering the backs of their heads. The room went suddenly silent.

The kakrow right above Tufan began to speak. 'Welcome to Endgame!' he rasped. 'Four games to win, four riddles to crack.'

The Taranauts crawled closer to each other in the dark, their faces to the ground, listening intently.

'Game One—SeeZee, also known as Seasliths and Zipcalators—Game of Chance—*Solo*.

'Game Two—Latang—Game of Skill—*Solo*.

'Game Three—BrainDrain—Game of Quick Thinking—*Solo*.

'Game Four—Bel Nolo—Game of Hand-Eye Coordination—*Teams of Three*.'

The kakrow paused. 'Game one—report tomorrow at 9 o'ding sharp with your champion. Shudder Bazaar SeeZee Indoor Stadium. Only three past the turnstiles.'

There was a sharp metallic clink as something dropped to the floor quite close to where the Taranauts lay huddled on the floor.

Then, with a great rush of giant wings and a raucous medley of cawing, the flock of kakrows was gone.

Zarpa came out of her crouch cautiously, blinking in the brightness of the arcalamps. A glittery purple ball lay on the floor a little distance away. She pounced on it with a shout, twisting it open. Out fell three shining purple stars on silver lanyards, and a tightly wound palmyra scroll.

'Our access stars!' cried Zvala, slinging one around her neck. Zarpa and Tufan grabbed the other two. 'Now let's see what's on the scroll . . .'

'Taranauts, Taranauts!' The Marani's voice was a little shaky. She had sat frozen in her chair throughout the kakrow episode, but now she was ready to take charge again. 'It's only ten dinglings to fliptime. Off to your rooms now—no arguments, please. We meet again here at 3 o'ding.'

'Of course, your Starness,' Zarpa thrust the scroll into her backsack and raced off, Zvala following close behind. 'Before you get any ideas,' she called to Tufan, 'I'm taking SeeZee!'

'Sure!' grinned Tufan. 'I've absolutely no interest in board games. I had my eye on Latang, actually—I am the gizmo freak, remember?'

'That's why I love you guys!' Zvala tossed over her shoulder cheerfully. 'The only game that sounded like fun to me was BrainDrain.'

The Marani watched them go, her face a mask of worry. Did the Taranauts really believe that these were mere *games*, that winning them would be that easy, or straightforward? Knowing Shaap Azur, she was pretty certain that he would set up a hard contest—a *battle*—with some mean surprises thrown in. She shivered involuntarily.

Snuggling under the soft razuvet in her comfy bed, Zarpa shivered, too. She had bravely volunteered to play the first game, but that was because she was sure she would go insane if she had to sit around doing nothing for yet another octite. *Winning*, however, was a completely different kettle of meenmaach. SeeZee was a game of chance—the probability that she would win against her unknown opponent was no more than half!

Six

'Shudder Bazaar SeeZee Indoor Stadium,' announced the cabamba driver.

The Taranauts hopped off. Zarpa's dad had wanted to drive them to the stadium, but Zarpa had flatly refused to let him. She felt he would make her nervous. In any case, the kakrow had been very clear that only three mithyakos would be allowed into the stadium. Taking a deep breath, she passed her access star over the blinking purple dot at the turnstile and entered the immense, high-ceilinged hall.

'Weee-ow!' said Zvala, taking in the hundreds of SeeZee grids painted on the floor. She grabbed a pair of stick dice and hopped on to a Start square. Rubbing the sticks together, she sent them spinning high into the air. The dice landed at her feet—one showed a four, the other a one. 'Five,' said Zvala, jumping five places.

'Zipcalator—yayyy!' She quickly ran up the painted zipcalator, reaching Square 25 in a jiffy.

'May I? May I?' begged Tufan. Zvala handed over the dice. Tufan spun them expertly into the air. This time, when they landed, one die showed a six and the other a three. 'Nine!' called Tufan. Zvala jumped nine places, and straight into a seaslith's mouth. 'Bummer!'

Tufan cheered. Zvala stuck her tongue out at him and ran down the seaslith's winding body to Square 12—into a very angry Zarpa.

'If you are both quite done with the fun and games,' she said tersely, 'perhaps you can help me figure out which board I am supposed to be playing on. We have a few stars to rescue, you know.'

Zvala reddened. 'Of course,' she said, looking around for Tufan to share the blame with. But the cunning lomdox was already far away, pretending to be very interested in a particular SeeZee board.

'I would imagine it is this one,' called Tufan, pointing to the massive SeeZee board at his feet. It was the largest one in the stadium, and bang under the big dome in the centre of the ceiling. 'This is where the finals of any SeeZee championship would be usually held, right?'

'Yes, that's Centre Board,' said Zarpa, walking across with Zvala. 'But . . .' she looked around, 'where is my opponent? And the dice?' She stopped suddenly, her body tensing. 'Uhhh . . . hang on a dingling, what's that?'

A low rumbling, like distant thunder, had begun below their feet. Then the ground began to shudder and shift. 'Get off the board!' yelled Tufan, leaping backwards. The sound got louder and louder and closer and closer, sounding very much like the Magmalift just before it took off.

Centre Board exploded out of the ground, shattering into millifragments. The giant dust cloud swirled and howled around the stadium, obscuring everything in sight.

Stick dice from all the other SeeZee boards flew into the maelstrom. 'Ow!' cried Zvala, as a die smacked hard into her face. 'Take cover!'

Five dinglings later, all was quiet. The Taranauts opened their eyes cautiously. 'What in Kay Laas . . .' started Tufan, but no other words would come. The others stared, equally dumbstruck.

In the middle of the stadium, where Centre Board had been, was a ginormous jungle gym that would have looked right at home in a giant's playground. It was a perfect cube, a 10 by 10 by 10 grid of strong metal bars that crisscrossed each other at regular intervals to create one hazillion smaller cubes. From random intersections, zipcalators sped upwards, humming busily.

'Um . . . Zarpa? It . . . it looks like you will be playing *three-dimensional* SeeZee,' stuttered Zvala. 'But . . . where are the seasliths?'

The words were barely out of her mouth when the hissing began. Out of the pit in the ground below the SeeZee frame came the seasliths, their long, sleek bodies glistening fatly in the light of the arcalamps. Each was as thick as three well-built mithyakos, and their scaly dun-coloured skins were slippery with slime. Fangs dripping venom curved malevolently out of fixed upper jaws, while hinged lower jaws opened wide enough to swallow a mithyakin whole. As the Taranauts watched in horrified fascination, the seasliths slithered lazily up the bars of the frame to their positions, their three-tined tongues flicking in and out. Then they yawned, lay their

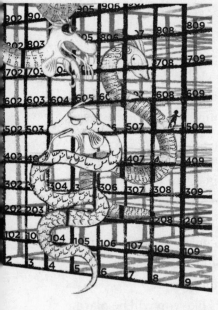

heads down on the metal bars, and went still.

The Taranauts looked at each other. The fun and games were most certainly over.

Zarpa took a deep breath. 'The dice.' It came out as an unintelligible squeak. She cleared her throat and hugged herself hard to stop the shivering. 'The dice, please!' she demanded of the SeeZee grid. 'Also, my opponent—whoever you are, show yourself!'

There was a misty shimmering on either side of the grid. As the Taranauts watched, a pair of stick dice, each as tall as Tufan, appeared on one side. On the other emerged a mammoth sandinger, its bottom half filled about three-quarters of the way with shining purple sand.

'A sandinger?' wondered Tufan. 'What's a sandinger doing in a SeeZee game?'

'I guess we'll figure it out,' said Zarpa, looking over the giant dice with a worried frown. 'What I'm wondering is how I will spin these and play at the same time!'

'Maybe Tufan and I can spin them,' offered Zvala, bending to pick them up. 'Uffpah! No way—I can't even budge them a centinch. Spinning them is completely out of the question.'

They exchanged worried glances. What now? They walked around the sandinger, craning their necks up at it, checking to see if there were any instructions on it.

Tufan began to walk backwards, keeping the sandinger in sight—maybe they were looking at it from the wrong angle. All of a sudden, he gave a loud yell. 'Watch out!' he cried. 'The sandinger—it's falling—run!'

Zarpa grabbed Zvala's hand and zipped swiftly away in her Obverse nanos. The sandinger fell with a deafening thud, then flipped itself so that the sand was now in the top half. As they watched, it began to drop into the empty bottom half in a thin steady stream.

'Zarpa!' yelled Zvala, as it suddenly struck her. 'There is no opponent! You are playing against the sandinger, against *time*! If you don't reach the last cube before the sand runs out, you lose! Hurry!'

Zarpa dropped her backsack and raced to the starting cube, patting her pockets to make sure the Born-Again Bars were there. She was ready to go, but unless someone figured out a way to spin the dice, how would she know where to jump to? 'I'm going to try jumping to the next cube,' she called out. An instant later, she came flying back, landing with a sickening thud. 'The grid is repulsified!' she groaned. 'Do something, guys!'

'Aaaaargh!' Tufan smacked his fist into his palm, keeping an eye on the sandinger.

'I wish we could figure out how to make these dice go UP!'

At the sound of the word, the pair of dice rose into the air. Tufan looked completely stunned. 'That's it!' he cried a dingling later. 'They're voice-activated! Watch this—SPIN!'

The dice spun in the air. 'DOWN!' yelled Tufan. The dice landed. 'A three and a four,' called Tufan. 'Seven!'

Zarpa jumped cautiously to the first cube. Nothing. It was safe. Quickly, she zigzagged to cube 7.

'UP!' called Tufan again. 'SPIN! DOWN! A six and a one. Seven again!'

'Which way?' called Zarpa. 'Do I finish the entire bottom level first or climb now?'

'No way of knowing,' said Zvala. 'But I would go with bottom level first.'

Zarpa reached the end of the row she was on, turned left, and put a foot out gingerly to test for repulsification. Nothing happened. 'Okay, we're on the right track,' she called out, as she zipped to cube 14.

Half a ding ticked by. Zarpa had gone through levels 1 and 2 without incident, and had just completed level 3. She had missed a few zipcalators on the way, but that was the way the game went. Now, however, things were going to get much more complicated.

The next spin of the dice would take her to level 4. She braced herself—if the dice came up six, she would encounter her first seaslith! She planned her move carefully. The important thing was to get past the seaslith before it roused itself, or she would be in serious danger. On the ground, Zvala crossed her fingers, chanting 'Not six, please, not six.'

'A one and a one,' said Tufan. Zarpa hoisted herself into level 4, and jumped two places. Tufan spun the dice again. 'A three,' called Tufan in a small voice, 'and a one.'

The worst had happened. Zarpa took a deep breath and prepared to slide down the seaslith as quietly as she possibly could.

BRRRRRRINGGG! Zarpa jumped out of her skin. It was the loudest alarm she had ever heard. The metal climbing frame vibrated like a live thing at the sound, and all the seasliths came wide awake at once, hissing and spitting!

Seven

Zarpa stayed where she was for a dingling, shivering violently. Way below, Zvala clutched Tufan, wishing there was some way she could help her friend. 'Zarpa!' cried Tufan. 'Stretch!'

Zarpa nodded. Locking her feet around the bar she was standing on, she began to stretch. Avoiding the repulsified bars, she wound and twisted her way through the cubes, back to level 3. The seaslith lashed out wildly, trying to keep her in its sight, but Zarpa was too quick. By the time the seaslith realized what was happening, she had jumped on to its back and slid quickly down to its tail. The seaslith hissed in frustration. Then, after making sure that there was no one on its level any more, it laid its head down and promptly fell asleep again.

'Nice work!' cheered Tufan. 'Keep going!'

He sent the dice spinning in the air again. 'A four and a six,' he called.

Zarpa zipped ten squares and reached level 3 for the second time. 'A six and a six! Hurray! Zipcalator!' Panting, Zarpa hopped on the zipcalator and leaned against its side, taking a bite out of a Born-Again Bar. With fresh energy coursing through her, she stepped off the zipcalator at level 6 and waved. 'Just four more levels!' she exulted, pumping her fists in the air.

But just three throws of the dice later, the alarm went off again. This time, the seaslith was just two squares away! It lunged for her face, its mouth so close that she could smell its stinking breath! Zarpa locked her feet around the bar and threw herself backwards, so that she hung upside down like a bat. Once again, she wove through the maze of repulsified bars until she was stretched to her full capacity. Just when her shoulders felt like they would pop out of their joints, she grabbed the seaslith's slippery back and released her feet. The seaslith thrashed about, trying to throw its assailant off, smacking her into the bars. Bruised and battered, Zarpa held on for dear life, until she finally slip-slid down the seaslith's tail to the right cube.

Dinglings ticked by. As the level in the top half of the sandinger fell, the sand began to drain out faster and faster. So far, Zarpa had not stopped or rested at all, but she hadn't made any real progress. There seemed to be more seasliths than zipcalators at every level, and she was beginning to despair of ever making it to the top. She was exhausted—her bruises hurt, every muscle ached terribly, and the Born-Again Bars were simply not doing enough.

'A three and a three! Mega Zipcalator! Woohoo!' exulted Tufan. Zarpa felt a small surge of hope—Mega Zipcalator would take her to level 9 for the very first time in the game. 'Do your thing, Tufan!' she yelled down from level 9 at the little speck that was Tufan. 'Anything but a twelve! There is a Megaseaslith waiting there!' She glanced anxiously at the rapidly emptying sandinger.

Tufan spun the dice. 'A six, and . . . a six,' he whispered, sinking to the ground in dismay. 'I'm sor. . .' The alarm screamed, drowning out the rest of his words. The seasliths came alive, hissing viciously.

'This isss sssso not fair!' cried Zarpa, all hope dribbling out of her as tears of frustration welled up in her eyes. 'Ssssssomeone help me! I'm ssssso tired!' She leaned her head against the nearest bar. She had failed her team, her parents, and all the Sparklkos. Now they'd never rescue the Amethysts, and it would all be her fault. She would just stay here forever, she decided, all alone, at the top of the grid. It was so calm here, so quiet . . .

Her head came up with a start. Calm? Quiet? Whatever happened to the hissing and spitting? Through her tears, she saw the blurry shape of the seaslith twelve squares away. So it was still here. Then what . . .? She looked down. From wherever they had been on the grid, the seasliths were snaking up to level 9. Zarpa stiffened, her heart beating a loud tattoo. What was this, a combined attack?

'Sssstop right there!' she yelled.

The seasliths kept on coming. Zarpa knew what she must do—lock feet, stretch, somersault, *something*—but her body wasn't listening. The sliths were all around her now, in great fat coils, their cold eyes staring unblinkingly at her, waiting . . .

'Here I am!' cried Zarpa. 'Sssso come and get me, you ssstinking sssslimy ssseasliths!'

The seasliths moved closer. Now their huge heads were centinches away from her feet. Zarpa closed her eyes tight, braced herself, and waited. It would all be over soon.

The hissing began again. It was a gentle hissing, and it seemed to have a certain pattern that repeated again and again.

Zarpa concentrated. It sounded like a . . . *word*, a word she knew!

'Ssssisssster,' hissed the seasliths. 'ssssissster.'

Zarpa's eyes flew open. Sister? But of *course*! She was the child of Shay Sha, the SuperSerpent, and so were the

seasliths! They had not known that she was one of them until her lisp had popped out and given her away. Zarpa began to laugh.

'Sssssistersss!' she crooned, throwing her arms and legs around the seasliths, her tiredness flying away from her like a flock of hakibyrds. 'My ssssisterssss!

Way down below, Zvala and Tufan were frantic with anxiety. Why were all the seasliths moving towards Zvala? Her body language screamed exhaustion—she needed help! They had run to the Start cube to try and reach her themselves, but every bar around it had been severely repulsified. Almost weeping from helplessness, Zvala upturned Zarpa's backsack—if nothing, she could toss her a Born-Again Bar. A portalamp came flying out, followed by a couple of empty wrappers, a bottle of water, a scratchscribe, a tightly wound scroll of palmyra . . .

Zvala stared at it. 'Tufan,' she said urgently, holding it up, 'we forgot about this.'

Tufan looked aghast. 'How *could* we?' he wailed, slapping his forehead. 'We need to crack this riddle to save Zarpa! Quick, what does it say?'

My first is in Shyn, and also in Lustr
My second is in flit, but not in flustr
My third is in meenmaach – a pair apart
To unlock a victory, that's where you start.
Now place me side by side with my twin
And shout it out loud for a glorious win!

'Tufan! Tuu-faaan!'

Tufan and Zvala whirled around at the sound of Zarpa's voice from the top of the grid.

'Spin the dice!' yelled Zarpa. She pointed to the sandinger. 'Quickly! Quickly!' She was standing twelve cubes away from where she had been, at the mouth of the waiting seaslith—only there was no seaslith there any more. All the seasliths were moving lazily about or slumbering in coils one level below, oblivious to Zarpa. Tufan and Zvala looked at each other and shrugged—they did not know how that had happened, but it was all good. 'You take the riddle, I'll spin the dice! Hurry!' said Tufan. 'UP!'

'You want me to solve the riddle *now*? What's the rush? Zarpa's almost done.'

'Wrong season for dumb questions!' snapped Tufan. 'Just do it!'

Promising herself that she would sock him good and proper once they were out of this creepy stadium, Zvala bent over the riddle with the scratchscribe and a papyrus pad. 'First is in Lustr *and* Shyn . . . that can only be S . . . Second in flit but *not* in fluster—not "f", not "l", not "t", so it has to be "i". Third is in meenmaach—a pair apart . . .'

Zvala looked puzzled. 'A pair apart—should I split up pair into 'pa' and 'ir'?' she muttered to herself. 'But neither is in meenmaach . . . Or is meenmaach a pair of words, meen and maach? No, I'm quite certain it is written as a single word . . .'

'She's made it! She's made it!' Tufan danced a merry jig around Zvala.

'Eeeeeeeee!' shrieked Zvala, jumping to her feet.

'Tufan! Zvala!' Zarpa was waving to attract their attention. 'Can't get into the End cube—there is a door but it's locked!'

'See? See?' Tufan turned on Zvala. 'I *told* you the riddle was important. I bet the door is voice-activated too, like the dice, and the word that unlocks it is the answer to the riddle! Have you got it yet?'

'No! I'm stuck—come over quick and help me!'

'A pair apart?' Tufan's brow furrowed. 'A pair usually means two identical things, so if we're talking about a pair of letters in meenmaach, say, it could mean "ee" or "aa" . . .'

'Or m and m—which are a pair of identical letters that . . . are not next to each other—'a pair apart'! That means we have S, I, M—SIM. Tufan, you're a genius!'

'I thought that was *obvious*,' shrugged Tufan. 'Okay, what next?'

'"Now place me side by side with my twin"—the only twins we know of are ShoonYa and Shaap Azur, but that's obviously not it . . .' Zvala pinched her lower lip.

'Hurry! Hurry! We're almost out of time!' yelled Zarpa. Zvala sneaked a quick glance—the last of the purple sand was beginning to trickle into the bottom of the sandinger!

'"Place me" . . .' read Tufan again. 'Who is *me*? Who are we talking about?'

'"Me" is the word—the word SIM. Remember how it began—"*My* first is in Lustr"?'

'Okay, so "my twin" must be . . .'

'SIM again!' cried Zvala and Tufan together. 'Zarpa! Zarpaaa! Try SIMSIM, whatever that means! You have to shout it out, really loud!'

'SIMSIM!' shouted Zarpa at the top of her voice. 'SIMSIM!' The door shimmered and disappeared.

'Made it!' Zarpa leaped into the air and wrapped her arms around the top bar of the End cube at exactly the same moment that the last few grains of sand fell to the bottom of the giant sandinger.

Instantly, from somewhere beyond the horizon, a shining purple star shot high into the sky with a *whooooosh!*, leaving a trail of lilac Taradust in its wake. The first Amethyst was free!

Eight

'Any news about the Latang game yet?' Zarpa walked into the breakfast room at the Marani's residence, looking well rested. The previous evening, she had chosen to go home instead of rooming with Zvala at the Marani's. Mama had fed her hot dalbroths, rubbed her aching body down with healing oils and tucked her into bed at 'nite. Papa had only shaken her hand formally, as if she was no longer a mithyakin now, and had smiled and smiled and smiled.

'Hey!' Zvala ran to her friend. 'You're looking *so* much better now!'

'That's right, *Zarpy!*' chortled Tufan, high-fiving her. 'Welcome back!'

Zarpa reddened. 'I asked if you had had any news about the next game,' she said quickly.

'Well, yes,' Tufan said, picking up the Hummonica lying on the table and smoothing it onto Zarpa's forehead. 'This was slipped under my door sometime this morning. How anyone besides the Marani knew that *I* would be the Latang player is anyone's guess . . .'

'Krrraaak!' The kakrow croaked straight into Zarpa's head. 'Game Two—Lunascoot Latang—report with your champion at 10 o'ding SHARP or your opponent gets a walkover. The match will be played at the sports field behind the . . .' A piece of music began to play. There was nothing more.

Zarpa frowned, peeling off the Hummonica. 'Lunascoot Latang? What's that?'

'Who knows?' shrugged Tufan, cutting himself his fourth monster wedge of chocolate galumpie. 'After 3-D SeeZee, anything is possible.'

'Actually,' said Zarpa, looking sheepish. 'I'm not even sure what normal Latang is. Gizmotronic games are just not my scene.'

'Oh, it's fairly simple,' said Zvala, trying to sound casual. Until the previous evening, she had had no idea at all of how the game was played. But after Zarpa had left with her dad, she had waited until Tufan was safely in the shower before she snuck into the Marani's library and dug out a wikipad on Latang. Now, in theory at least, she was a champion Latangler.

She pulled out a pad and her scratchscribe. 'First, you shoot a conetop into the air with a Latangun, see? Then, before it can fall to the ground, you quickly lock the infraglo beam from the Latangun with the conetop receiver. Then you use the freewheeling joystick—which, by the way, can move right, left, front, back, and in a circle—to control the conetop's movements—direction, height, spin . . .'

'Exactly,' said Tufan, giving Zvala's illustration an approving look. Very few girls he knew would have been able to explain the game so precisely. 'In the meanwhile, your opponent has gone through the same motions. So his conetop is also in the air. The object of the game is to slice your opponent's infraglo beam with yours, and eventually knock his conetop out.'

'While of course,' finished Zvala, 'you make sure he doesn't knock *your* conetop out!' She raised an inquiring eyebrow. 'Got that?'

'So-ort of,' said Zarpa doubtfully. 'But how do you "knock out" your opponent's conetop?'

'Well, once your beam and your opponent's have crossed, they lock together,' explained Zvala. 'But to keep your beam locked in that position, you need to hold your joystick in place and make absolutely, absolutely sure that it does not move even a teensy-weensy bit. Every time your joystick jiggles, your opponent's beam gets stronger by a certain number of watvolts. And vice versa. Once one player's beam's strength touches a hazillion watvolts, the other's conetop gets knocked out.'

Zarpa nodded slowly, glancing at her dingdial. 'Oh-kay. I don't have it all yet, but I'll figure it out when we get there.' She gathered up her backsack.

'And where precisely are you going, Zarpy?' Tufan raised one eyebrow at her.

'Oh,' Zarpa slapped her forehead. 'The kakrow didn't actually say where, did it?'

'Exactly,' shrugged Tufan. 'We've listened to what's on the Hummonica loads of times already—"The match will be played at the sports field behind the . . ."' He hummed the piece of music. 'There's nothing more.'

'Is the music drowning out something the kakrow said?' asked Zarpa.

'I don't think so,' said Zvala. 'The kakrow actually stops talking at "'the".'

'Maybe the *music* is the clue!' said Zarpa excitedly. 'Maybe that's our second riddle.'

'Bri-lli-ant!' said Zvala slowly. 'If it *is* part of a song, maybe the answer is in the name of the song, or the name of the composer, or singer, or something . . . .'

'Doesn't hurt to try and find out!' Tufan hummed the tune in his head, and touched the search icon on the Hummonica. Three dinglings later, the Hummonica had finished searching its vast memory banks and returned a disappointing 'No matches found'.

'Maybe if we break it down into the individual notes using the "Notate" feature?' ventured Tufan, touching the Notate icon and humming the tune again. The notes began to scroll across his forehead. Tufan peeled off the Hummonica and began to copy the notes down on a papyrus pad.

'Do-La-Fa-Mi,' he wrote. 'Fa-Mi-Mi-Re-Fa-La-Do-Mi. That's it.'

The three of them stared down at the notes. 'Is there someplace called the Dolafami in Sparkl, Zarpa?' asked Zvala.

Zarpa shook her head. 'And before you ask, neither is there any place called Famimire or Faladomi.'

They burst out laughing. Then Zarpa glanced at her dingdial. 'Just one ding for the match to begin and we don't even know where to go yet! I don't want the other guy to get a walkover! Focus!'

'Hey!' said Zvala, her eyes shining. 'Aren't musical notes also named by the letters of the alphabet? C for Do, D for Re, and so on? I did a basic harpiano course in school once and I remember learning it that way.'

'You're right!' said Tufan, beginning to write again. 'It goes this way.'

C   D   E   F   G   A   B
Do Re Mi Fa So La Ti

'So if we substitute letters for the notes, we get . . .

CAFEFEEDFACE. Does that make any sense to you?'

'Café Feedface!' yelled Zarpa. 'It's a rundown little place too close to the Downside, so no one really goes there much. But yes, there's a huge field behind it. Let's go—I know exactly where it is!'

Slinging their access stars around their necks, the Taranauts raced to the waiting cabamba. Tufan's backsack bulged with powertein-packed puffboos, Born-Again Bars, fruity vigorshake karrypaks, vita-fortified imlichi bubblechews—after seeing how exhausted Zarpa had gotten yesterday, he was taking no chances. He wondered guiltily how Makky was doing. He was certainly being looked after well, the star attraction at the Sparkl Animal Care Centre, visited every waking dingling by scores of little Sparklkins, but . . . He promised himself he would look in on him this evening, after the game.

After the game . . . Tufan had a sudden sinking feeling in the pit of his stomach—he knew for a fact that he was a decent Latangler, but who knew what Lunascoot Latang was about?

Could he really pull off another win for the Taranauts?

'There's the lunascoot!' Zvala called out, racing towards it across the field behind Café Feedface. 'And look! It is custom-built—it has the Latangun mounted on the dashboard!'

'Hmm,' Tufan walked around the lunascoot, examining it closely. 'Does that mean I have to drive this around when

I play, instead of simply standing on the ground as I usually do?'

'Do you even know how to?' asked Zarpa. 'Drive this, I mean?'

'Well, I've never driven it on the streets, of course—I'm too young to have a licence,' admitted Tufan. 'But Dada taught me how to drive one last octon, so I should be able to manage it.'

Tufan jumped on and pressed the start button. The engine coughed and vroomed into life. But the lunascoot did not move. 'The speed-up lever is missing,' he said, puzzled. 'I wonder what these pedals are for . . .' He pressed down hard on the middle pedal. The next instant, the lunascoot had shot off skywards like a rocket!

'Haaaaaalp!' he screamed, hastily taking his foot off the pedal. The lunascoot began to plummet to the ground! The girls squealed in panic. Once again, Tufan pressed down on the pedal. He took off again.

'Try another pedal!' yelled Zarpa. Tufan pressed down on the left pedal. The lunascoot banked steeply left and tilted at a crazy angle, beginning to drop fast again. Tufan pressed one pedal after another, fighting for control. The lunascoot careened wildly across the treetops.

'Feet off the pedals!' The high-pitched little voice spoke straight into Tufan's ear. Tufan took his feet off the pedals.

The lunascoot righted itself immediately, but began to fall like a stone. 'Left thumb on the pause button on the dashboard!' tweeted another high-pitched voice in his other ear. Tufan scanned the dashboard for the pause button and brought his left thumb down on it hard. Instantly, the lunascoot stopped falling and stood absolutely still, suspended in midair.

'Uffffffpah!' breathed Tufan, wiping his sweating brow. 'Thanks, guys, whoever you are—you're lifesavers!'

'You're welcome!' squeaked two little voices. Tufan whirled—hovering in midair on their flying lunascoots, grinning from ear to ear, were the two minimits the Taranauts had once captured in the Mayazaal!

Tufan goggled. 'How . . .?'

The minimits tittered sharply and pointed to the ground below. Standing there, grunting excitedly and prancing around like a makarakin, was Makky. Next to him, his indigo-and-gold threaded braid jiggling as he guffawed at the flabbergasted look on Tufan's face, was Zub!

Nine

'Welcome to the Lunascoot Latang play-offs!' blared the volumizers around the field. 'Best-of-three format. Players, present yourselves!'

Tufan walked to the centre of the Latang field, Zarpa and Zvala close behind him. With the minimits' expert inputs, he had a pretty good idea now of how to manoeuvre the lunascoot. Of course, he had had very little practice, but having Zub and Makky appear so unexpectedly had sent his spirits and his confidence soaring. Quickly, he ran the lunascoot controls over in his mind—middle pedal to gain and lose height quickly, left pedal to turn 90 degrees left, right one to turn 90 degrees right. Left-right arrows on dashboard for finer turns, advance-reverse buttons to move forwards and back, up-down arrows to gain and lose height in small preset amounts. Pause button to hover.

'There he comes!' whispered Zarpa.

A young pale-skinned mithyaka was jogging down the field from the other end. His curly hair was ash-blond, his limbs lean and wiry.

'Harharazur!' he said grimly, his heels snapping to attention. Closer up, he towered over the Taranauts, and they could see that his hooded eyes were a startling shade of mauve. 'Mog Ambow, Champion Lunascoot Latangler of the Downside, greets you. Only one way this game can end—I win, you lose.'

'Oh, hello yourself!' returned Tufan. 'I'm Tufan—and good luck to you, too!'

Zvala giggled. Mog Ambow's face flushed red and twisted in anger. 'Snicker all you want, cheekypants!' he growled. 'We'll see who's laughing at the end of the game!' He turned and strode rapidly to where his lunascoot waited.

Tufan handed over Squik and Chik-Chik to Zarpa. Then all three walked over to where Makky and Zub stood guarding the lunascoot. 'He will be trying his best to lock into your infraglo beam immediately, but don't let him,' advised Zub. 'Just play with him for a bit— figure out his strengths and weaknesses, try and gauge how good he really is.'

'Got that!' nodded Tufan.

'We'll be flying right by you,' squeaked the minimits. 'And telling you which controls to use when.'

'Oh no, you won't!' said Tufan, horrified. 'That's cheating!'

'Oh, come on, Tufan!' protested Zvala. 'Mog already has a huge advantage over you—he is a "champion Lunascoot Latangler", and you only ever rode your first flying lunascoot about half a ding ago! And it isn't as if the minimits will be actually *flying* your lunascoot . . .'

'Whatever,' said Tufan firmly. 'That's still cheating. Now wish me luck, all of you!'

Helmeted and strapped securely into their seats, the players faced each other across the field and revved their engines. 'Ready,' a voice boomed through the helmet Hummonicas, 'get set . . . and GO!'

Both the lunascoots rose straight into the air. 'Shoot!' Spinning madly, two conetops—one black, the other silver, shot out of the Latanguns and zigzagged towards each other. Quickly, Tufan pressed the pause button, then released the infraglo beam. Steering the Latangun expertly, he aimed the beam at his spinning conetop, following its crazy unpredictable course closely until, with a shrill beep, it locked with the receiver. With his right hand, he grabbed the joystick—he was now in control of his conetop.

'Yayyyy!' cheered Zvala and Zarpa! 'Go, Tufan! Go, black conetop!'

Tufan looked over at his opponent. Mog had locked his beam into his conetop several dinglings ago, and was now yawning exaggeratedly. 'Done all you could, little mithyakin?' he taunted, his fingers resting lightly on his joystick. 'Now watch the fun!'

In the next instant, before Tufan could blink, Mog had pushed his joystick forward and brought his beam within a millinch of Tufan's! If Tufan didn't move his beam immediately, he would be locked as soon as the game had begun.

Tufan whipped the Latangun to the left. The beam, with the conetop at its end, sped away to the left. Mog swivelled his lunascoot right and sped forward, always keeping his Latangun focused on the black conetop. Tufan panicked, pressing down on the middle and left pedals at the same time. The lunascoot shot up, leaning so sharply left  at the same time that it lost balance and turned horizontal, skidding in the air. Tufan yelled in fright.

'Muhahahaha!' Mog cackled uproariously into Tufan's head, bringing his lunascoot smoothly to Tufan's level and beginning the chase again. 'How far will the poor little mithyakin run? How long?'

Tufan thought fast—Mog was obviously a much better lunascooterist than he would ever be. His own best chance was to move the lunascoot as little as possible and concentrate instead on the Latangun itself. Pulling on his joystick, he angled his beam upwards and swung the Latangun in a wide, smooth arc so that it was now all the way around the other side from where Mog was. Mog swore and began to reverse rapidly. The moment Mog was in locking range again, Tufan angled the beam sharply down and swivelled the Latangun around. The conetop was now almost directly below him.

Sputtering with anger, Mog began to back up and drop height at the same time. Tufan grinned to himself. This was working—he hadn't moved the lunascoot at all, and he had already led Mog a merry dance. 'Enjoying your morning flyaround, Mog?' he mocked.

'Harharazur!' yelled Mog, changing direction and coming straight at Tufan as if he meant to crash into him! For an instant, Tufan went blank. Then he grabbed the joystick and pulled on it, adeptly manoeuvring the infraglo beam straight into the onrushing Mog's. The beams locked. Instantly, the black and silver conetops at

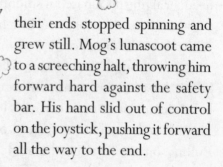

their ends stopped spinning and grew still. Mog's lunascoot came to a screeching halt, throwing him forward hard against the safety bar. His hand slid out of control on the joystick, pushing it forward all the way to the end.

'Black conetop beam at a hazillion watvolts and climbing,' announced the voice. 'Game over. Black conetop wins. Score 1–0.'

Below, Zarpa, Zvala and Zub turned triumphant cartwheels. Pleased that his favourite mithyakins seemed happy, Makky joined in the excitement, grunting loudly and rolling in the mud.

'Game two! Ready, set, and . . . go!'

Once again, the two lunascoots rose into the air. The black and silver conetops spun swiftly out of the Latanguns and engaged quickly with their infraglo beams. Once again, Mog rushed to lock his beam with Tufan's. This time, Tufan was more confident and ready for him. Getting a firm hold of his joystick, he rotated it round and round. The beam kept pace, inscribing large rapid circles in the air in a dizzying blur, driving Mog nearly insane as he tried to intercept it.

Then, suddenly, more out of sheer luck than any planned strategy, Mog managed to bring his beam in the path of Tufan's. The beams locked. It was now a game of concentration and stillness. Dinglings ticked away. Neither Mog nor Tufan had moved their joysticks a millinch. Tufan copped a quick glance at the dashboard timer. Another three dinglings and the game would time out, resulting in a draw. He thought of Achmentor Achalmun and made his body go perfectly still, as he had been taught, determined to last it out without giving away a single watvolt.

On the other lunascoot, Mog bent down and fiddled with something under his seat. Tufan wondered what he was up to. As he watched, a little hatch opened in the front of the lunascoot.

WHUMP! Out of nowhere, a screaming high-velocity headwind slammed into Tufan like a brick wall. Locked hard to the beam, the lunascoot bucked like an aquauto in a storm-tossed sea, bouncing him around and banging him into the safety bars. Momentarily stunned, Tufan let go of the joystick, leaving it to the mercy of the wind. The joystick slip-slid swiftly all the way to the back.

'Silver conetop beam at a hazillion watvolts and climbing,' announced the voice. 'Game over. Silver conetop wins. Score 1–1.' The last thing Tufan heard before twisting his helmet off and throwing it to the ground was Mog's delighted cackling.

'The crooked, conniving lomdox!' Zvala stamped her foot indignantly, her face already a flaming scarlet. 'I'm sure he had a turbo galeblower concealed somewhere on that lunascoot!'

Zarpa was equally furious. 'Now that we don't have to play fair any more, let's pull out the stops! Tufan, use your powers—blow Mog away to the ends of Mithya!'

Tufan shook his head. 'He will be expecting that—probably has some kind of windshield around him. But,' his eyes grew dark, 'Mog'd better watch out anyway—I'm ready to play dirty now!'

It was ten dinglings into the crucial game—whoever won this would win the contest. Tufan's mind was on high alert, watching for the slightest false move his opponent might make. His body was taut as a bowstring, bracing itself for nasty surprises from any direction. Once again, he was making Mog run circles around him. But this time, Mog didn't seem to mind that much—he remained infuriatingly smug, as if he knew he was going to win.

It was just before the beams locked that it happened.

Tufan had been rotating the joystick again, and Mog had been flying high and low trying to intercept it. Then, all of a sudden, the joystick began going round in the opposite direction. Puzzled, Tufan rotated it back in the right direction. The joystick slipped away from the circular groove and moved into the right-left groove. Tufan guided it back onto the circular groove again. Once again, the joystick slipped out and moved into the front-back groove. It seemed to have a mind entirely its own.

'Having trouble, little mithyakin?' smirked Mog through the helmet Hummonica. Tufan began to sweat. This was it! Now Mog would lock the beams together and there would be no way Tufan would be able to control the joystick and keep it still. He had already lost!

'Tufan!' Zub's voice, speaking straight into his head, was calm and unhurried. 'Listen to me—try Stellikinesis!'

'I . . . I can't!' stammered Tufan, wondering at the same time how Zub had managed to access the helmet Hummonica. 'I'm completely useless at it . . .'

'Nonsense!' Zarpa was speaking now, equally calm. 'Absolute focus, Tufan, absolute focus.'

'Aaaaaa . . . uuuuu . . . mmmm.' As Zarpa and Zvala intoned the Chant of Deep Stillness, Tufan felt himself grow quiet and composed. With the calmness came three clear thoughts—Mog had not played fair and he did not deserve to win. If Mithya had to be saved, the Amethysts had to be rescued. And if he, Tufan, did not win this game, that would not happen.

Beeep! Mog had locked his beam with Tufan's. There was no time to lose. Tufan's joystick was still motionless, but he knew it could start moving anytime. He focused hard on the joystick, willing it to stay put. The joystick began to move. 'Silver conetop beam at one centillion watvolts!' said the referee's voice. Tufan focused harder. He could feel the resistance from the joystick—he was doing it!

He sneaked a glance at Mog, who looked satisfactorily baffled, and lost his concentration for an instant. The joystick slipped a couple of millinches. 'Silver at four centillion!' Tufan kicked himself mentally and focused again. Once again, the joystick moved a little. 'Silver at seven centillion!' Tufan broke out in a sweat and doubled his concentration.

On the other lunascoot, Mog was running out of patience by the dingling. What was going *on*? This game should have been over a long time ago! He cursed the Demazur who had forced him to play this match, assuring him that his opponent was a fumbling amateur. Obviously, the Demazur had not done his homework. This unseeded, unheard-of young mithyakin had given him a stiff fight. What was more, thought Mog with a little twinge of admiration, he had given him a fair fight.

'Finish him now, Mog!' The Demazur screamed into Mog's head. 'Lose this match, and the consequences are not going to be happy!' Mog stiffened. He could not let the mithyakin win! However, the tampered joystick did not seem to be doing its job. He would just have to use the galeblower again and end this thing quickly.

Out of the corner of his eye, Tufan saw Mog bend again and felt fury rise within him. Still focusing on the joystick, he drew in a great breath of air, until his lungs were so full they felt like they would burst. Then he exhaled, letting it all go in one superstrong *Hoooo*! Mog reared backwards with the impact, his hand slipping off the joystick.

'Black conetop beam at a hazillion watvolts and climbing! Score 2–1. Game and match, black conetop.'

Tufan stayed suspended in midair for a little while, savouring the moment. It was over. He had won. The Taranauts had rescued another Amethyst. He could hear Zarpa and Zvala cheering at the top of their voices, but all he could think of was . . . the impossible had happened— *he had gotten the hang of Stellikinesis*! Woohoo! He couldn't wait to go back and tell Achalmun.

Mog stayed in midair too, his insides twisting as he imagined the awful consequences awaiting him. But that was how the Downside worked—the Demazurs ruled their people with an iron hand, controlling them through fear and terror. He straightened his shoulders—there was one small thing he *could* do before he went back to face the consequences. As Tufan watched, incredulous, Mog raised his fist to him in a sportsman's salute to a worthy opponent. Then he swung the lunascoot around and was gone.

'Well done, well *done*!' congratulated Zub, when Tufan had finally landed. Tufan felt a warm glow spread through him—it was so great to have Zub back. They both went into an elaborate Lustr Blasters' salute—chest-bump, back-bump, 'Brother!' war cry.

'An extraordinary achievement, Taranaut Tufan!' squealed Zvala and Zarpa, appearing suddenly on either side of him, thrusting imaginary micphones into his face. How do you feel?'

'Well, if you really want to know . . .' began Tufan, his eyes drifting shyly to the ground. Then he looked up. 'Hungry!' he yelled suddenly into their smiling faces. Picking up his loaded backsack, he hoisted himself on to Makky's back. 'Giddyap, boy!' he laughed, digging his heels into the makara's sides as the girls came after him, shaking their fists. 'Get me away from the paparazzi!'

Ten

Zvala had dressed carefully this morning—her 'lucky' lavender capris, a white peasant-girl blouse with violet flowers on the collar, and purple floaters painted over with tiny silver stars. Now, she unwrapped two Brainchow bars and added them to the wholegrain carbozest-laden protlees and powertein-packed scrambled mottegs on her already-laden breakfast platter. This morning of all mornings, she was going to eat right. Both Zarpa and Tufan had done the Taranauts proud—now it was her turn.

'No Hummonica message, no scroll falling out of the sky, nothing,' said Zarpa glumly. 'No indication at all yet of where you will play BrainDrain.'

'Oh, we'll get to know sooner or later, I imagine,' said Tufan, piling his plate high with oily batatfries and grabbing a couple of bottles of pepcofizz. 'But what *is* BrainDrain, exactly?'

'As far as I know,' shrugged Zarpa, taking her place at the table, 'it's a set of puzzles that you have to solve within a time limit. It should be a complete breeze for our Ms Brainiac.'

Zvala shook her head darkly. 'I'm sure there is an impossible-to-solve "For-Taranauts-Only" edition of the game, designed just for us by our dear Shaap Azur.'

She sat down, shook out her napkin, and smoothed it on her lap—her lucky capris were to be protected at all costs! 'Wonder who chose these napkins,' she murmured, picking up her fork. 'Really strange design.'

'What's strange about some dumb old flowers?' shrugged Tufan.

"Yeah. Mine has flowers too,' said Zarpa.

'Really?' Zvala pulled off her napkin. 'Don't your napkins look like this?'

Tufan and Zarpa shook their heads. 'That must be our riddle, then!' cried Zvala. 'Eat up, quickly, and we'll go figure it out!'

Ten dinglings later, comfortably stuffed, the Taranauts were peering down at the napkin, trying to make sense of its strange pattern of closely-packed thick and thin lines. As far as they could see, there were no words on it, no numbers, and certainly no instructions. They turned the napkin around this way and that, studied its reflection in Zvala's hand mirror, and held it against the light of the closest arcalamp. Nothing.

'Uffpah!' Tufan let out a frustrated sigh. The napkin floated up in the air and floated back on to the table. 'I have never felt so clueless in my life!'

He blew on the napkin again. It rose, a little higher this time. Tufan blew harder, making a game of keeping the napkin in the air. He blew it straight into Zarpa's face and then blew it away before she could grab it.

'Stop fooling around, Tufan!' snapped Zvala. 'That's our ticket to the third Amethyst! Bring the napkin down this instant!'

'Yes, your Starness!' Tufan bowed. 'Here you go!'

He blew the napkin to Zvala so that it floated in front of her face. Zvala made a grab for it. Tufan inhaled hard. The napkin zipped towards him.

'Oh, come *on*, Tufan! Don't be a sillykoof! This is serious,' scolded Zarpa, taking one look at Zvala's furious face. Tufan exhaled. The napkin floated right back to Zvala and hung there horizontally at eye level, buoyed from below by a gentle jet of Tufan's breath. 'Drop it, Tufan!' ordered Zarpa. Tufan stopped blowing. The napkin began to float down to the table.

'No!' yelled Zvala. 'Tufan, keep blowing! Bring it back to where it was, level with my eyes.' Tufan rolled his eyes. 'Make up your minds, guys!' But he did as Zvala said, and the napkin floated back up.

'There! That's perfect! Stop! Keep it there!' said Zvala. She closed one eye and concentrated on the pattern. 'I see it! I see letters!'

'Where?' chorused Zarpa and Tufan, running to her side and bending so that the napkin was level with their eyes.

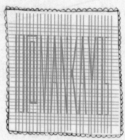

'TEN,' read Zvala. 'Then there is a @ symbol, which means AT.'

'And then there is a set of letters—M-A-N-K-A-Y-O-S, I think,' said Tufan. 'Mean anything to you?'

'Yes!' yelled Zarpa. 'It must mean the Manse of Mankayos—it is part of an old abandoned set of a starvision game show that used to be starcast when Papa and Mama were in school. There were puzzle pods in there, each with a different kind of puzzle, and to get from one pod to the other, you had to jump across things and swing from ropes and whatnot, and if you didn't finish the entire course in a specified time, you got locked in.'

Zvala gulped. The puzzle pods sounded like something she could handle, but swinging from ropes and jumping across things . . . 'Zarpa, do you want to take this game, too?' she asked in a small voice.

'Are you nuts?' said Zarpa. 'There's no way I'd be able to crack the puzzles within the given time. You are our best hope and you know it.'

'Our *only* hope,' corrected Tufan firmly. 'You are not as bad at Kalarikwon and rope-climbing as you used to be, you know,' he added magnanimously. 'You might just get your blue pants a little dirty, that's all.'

'Thanks a lot!' snapped Zvala. 'And they're *lavender*!'

'So where are we off to this two-Amethyst morning?' Zub walked in, bright-eyed and smiling. 'So that Taranaut Zvala can give us a three-Amethyst evening?'

'Don't be so sure about Amethyst Three, Zub,' sighed Zvala. 'BrainDrain sounds tough enough, and now I have to play it at the Manse of Mankayos!'

'You'll do fine!' said Zub reassuringly. 'If you make it to the Manse by 10 o'ding, that is . . .'

'Into the cabamba, everyone!' ordered Zarpa.

'You guys go on ahead. I'll follow you on the Makkybus,' called Tufan, running towards the Animal Care Centre.

Enormous, decrepit, and forbidding, the Manse of Mankayos stood at the edge of a long-abandoned amusement park, ringed by a sturdy stone wall. The top of the wall bristled with embedded shards of broken glass that glinted evilly in the light of the arcalamps, and the tall iron entrance gates were looped through with stout chains, now rusty with age. By the side of the gates was a mammoth sculpture of a grinning genie emerging from a lamp, its paint cracked and flaking. The wind howled through the empty window frames of the castle, scattering bubblechew wrappers and bits of ancient newspapyrus.

'A-are you s-sure that this is the p-place?' asked Zvala, fighting to keep her voice steady. 'Th-there are no lights inside.'

'And since when does the Child of Fire need lights, anyway?' chuckled Zub.

Zvala pulled her lilac scrunchie off her wrist, gathered her hair into a ponytail, and straightened her shoulders. Zub was right—she was being ridiculous. After all, she had special gifts and a very sharp brain. More importantly, Mithya needed her. She threw Zub a grateful smile, then strode up to the tall iron gates and shook them hard.

'Welcome to Mankayos!' The shrill voice seemed to come from somewhere inside the genie. Purple lights had gone on behind his eyes, and a purple dot blinked in his navel. 'Access star, please—single entry only.'

'That would be me,' said Zvala, passing her access star over the genie's navel. The chains fell to the ground with a heavy clink, and the gates swung open. 'Three puzzle pods to punch through,' intoned the genie. 'Game times out in two dings exactly.'

'Take my dingdial,' said Zarpa quickly. 'And keep an eye on the time. When there are ten dinglings left, concentrate on getting out, even if you haven't finished all the puzzles. Do you understand?'

Zvala nodded. She marched up the walkway to the big double doors and pounded on them. No answer. She tried the handle. The doors were securely locked, and the windows too high for her to climb through. 'Oh great, what now?' she muttered. It felt good to say things aloud, made her feel as if she wasn't alone. 'Go on, then, Mankayos,' she yelled. 'Throw whatever you have at me!'

With a beep, a panel slid silently open by the side of the double doors. Zvala stepped in. The door slid shut behind her. Suddenly the little room came alive with centillions of blinking lamps, and began to pulsate to a medley of high-pitched gizmotronic sounds. The entire floor turned into a giant backlit number keypad. Zvala stepped hurriedly away to its edge, and stood there on tiptoe, her back to the wall.

'The Digi Pod!' giggled the genie. 'Punch in the right combination to get out—and get in!' Zvala waited. '*Take the first fifty numbers—and,*' chanted the genie, '*add them all up where you stand. In one dingling—or you'll be banned.*'

Zvala thought quickly. However, did one add up the first fifty numbers in one dingling flat? If she went in order— $1+2 = 3$; $3+4 = 7$; $7+5 = 12$—it would take her dings and dings! There *was* another way—some trick she had learnt in one of Achmentor Achalmun's sessions, a short cut of some kind . . .

0	1	2	3	4	5	6	7	8
50	49	48	47	46	45	44	43	42

'Got it!' she yelled triumphantly, pulling out a palmpad and a scratchscribe as the memory kicked in. 'First divide fifty in half, that's 25,' she said aloud. 'Now write down the numbers from 0 to 25 in one line and the numbers 25 to 50 in a line below the first one in the opposite direction. Each pair of numbers in the two lines—0 & 50, 1 & 49, 2 & 48—adds up to 50. So basically, you have to add up 26 fifties, or half that many hundreds—and that makes . . . 1300!'

Now to punch them in! The numbers were so far apart—could she do it? Thinking of Twon d'Ung, Zvala launched herself into the air and landed bang in the middle of the '1' square. Yay! More confident now, she leaped again, onto '3'. Now came the big one. Bracing herself and sending up a prayer, Zvala took a flying leap towards '0' and made it with a millinch to spare! Then she jumped once again on the same square. The panel slid open.

Outside, the double doors creaked open on rusty hinges. Zvala stepped confidently over the threshold—and tumbled straight into a pit of freezing water! Instantly, the doors shut behind her, plunging everything into darkness!

Eleven

'Okay, that was smart!' Zvala chided herself as she paddled furiously, her flailing feet and arms groping blindly for a boundary wall. Finally, her arms locked around a wobbly ledge of some kind. Draping herself over it, Zvala raised her arm and got some fire going.

Blinking in the sudden brightness, she took stock of her surroundings. The 'ledge' she was lying on was actually a floating disc, one of a row of four leading from the main doors to the side of the narrow canal she had fallen into, where a batakoose-shaped pedal boat bobbed gently. A row of pillars flanked the canal, each with a sconce supporting an old-fashioned mashaalamp. Zvala sent a flame shooting towards one of them, wondering if it would catch. It blazed up immediately. Yes! Quickly, she lit as many as she could.

'Well, I'd better get started, I suppose,' she said loudly, hoisting herself into the boat and unhitching it from the post. A map of the canal was nailed to the dashboard. 'According to this, the Memory Pod is straight down and second left,' she said, steering out into the canal and beginning to pedal. 'Let's go!'

'Squik! Hey, Squik! Come back!'

But for once, the furry little gileli wasn't listening to Tufan. She had been nestling happily in his pocket until the doors of Mankayos closed behind Zvala. The moment they did, though, she had got the wind up. Leaping out of his pocket, she had darted away towards the Manse. Now she scurried up the front wall, climbed over a window sill, and vanished from sight.

'Well,' shrugged Tufan, 'maybe she smelt some of her cousins inside. She'll find her way back eventually. Come on, Makky, let's go for a ride.'

Zvala glanced at the dingdial on her wrist. A whole ding gone already and the Memory Pod was nowhere in sight. She had been pedalling furiously down the second left branch of the canal for ages now—her muscles ached and she was beginning to get anxious. But the black, oily water seemed to stretch forever.

Suddenly, the canal widened out into a vast circular lake. In the middle of the lake floated a perfect sphere with no doors or windows. Finally! She pedalled around it, until she spotted the blinking purple dot. A dingling later, she was inside the pod.

'The Memory Pad!' A giant genie appeared in front of Zvala, floating in the air like a luminous ghost. Zvala nearly cried out before she realized it was only a holographic projection. '*A dozen images high and low,*' shrilled the genie. '*Memorize, then lay out in a row. In order, mind, or prepare for woe.*'

Okay, she would nail this one! She had learnt how to remember a series of objects in order when she had started doing Ma's shopping by herself. Instead of writing down a shopping list, Ma had taught her a fun memory technique—link the first item on the list to the next one with a weird image, then link the second and third the same way, and so on. 'Bring them on, genie!' she called.

The holographic images began to flash in front of Zvala. An aquauto. A creposa. A Hummonica. A meenmaach. Megastage. A backsack. A mazikannakki plant. A hobgaram. A can of Max deo. The Magmalift. Shaap Azur.

A glass of purple plumberry flipfloat. Then all the images came back together for a dingling, and hovered blurry-edged in the still, stale air.

Zvala's brain went into overdrive, creating memory pictures that linked one image and the next. First image—aquauto. Second—creposa. What about an aquauto carrying a stack of creposas? Too normal. What about an

aquauto *eating* a creposa? Better. Or an aquauto surfing on a giant creposa? Perfect! Next. Creposa and Hummonica. The creposa sailed out of the water, and turned into a Hummonica? She imagined smoothing a mini-creposa on her forehead.

The story-links formed rapidly in her head. A meenmaach leaped out of the water and grabbed the Hummonica, smoothing it on its forehead. It zipped through the water and suddenly appeared on Megastage, crooning its favourite Dana Suntana number. A heavy backsack dropped out of the sky onto the meenmaach, ending its short-lived career as a rockstar. Around the backsack grew a shining field of Mazikannakki. When the annakki was ripe, the grains popped out and flew like little emeralds into the hobgarams impaled on the fence surrounding the field.

As they cooked, the stink of Max deo floated out of the hobgarams, polluting the atmosphere and sending maxphyxiating mithyakos hurrying towards the Magmalift to escape. Oh, no—inside the Magmalift was Shaap Azur! But did that scare the mithyakos? Of course not! They just dumped all their glasses of plumberry flipfloat on top of his head! Done!

The pod went dark. Zvala waited with bated breath for instructions, running the links over in her head. 'Recall,

please!' shrieked the genie. 'Here goes,' muttered Zvala. 'Aquauto!' she called. 'Creposa!' She hesitated. What was the third one? Something had happened to the creposa—oh yes, it had turned into a . . . 'Hummonica!' she yelled. 'Meenmaach! Megastage! Backsack! . . . Purple plumberry flipfloat!' she finished triumphantly.

The door slid open. Zvala jumped back into the boat, glancing at the dingdial. This was almost too easy. Just one more puzzle to crack and she was out of here!

Makky stopped suddenly, his snout working like a pair of bellows. Something did not smell right. 'What's up, boy?' said Tufan. 'Don't want to cross the water?' He and Makky had circled round to the back of Mankayos, and now stood at the edge of a sluggish stream winding out of the back gate of the castle. The water was inky and oily, and smelt foul, but for a strong swimmer like Makky, the stream was not a problem to cross. Something else was bothering him—was the water poisonous?

'Chik-chik, chik-chik!' A red and gold striped kipchali looked curiously up at Tufan from the grass. 'Chik-chik!' responded Tufan's kipchali, poking his head out of his pocket. The next instant, Chik-Chik had leapt out onto the grass. 'Hey, look, Makky, Chik-Chik has a new friend!' smiled Tufan. As they watched, the kipchalis raced towards the stream.

Makky began to whimper. 'Hey, Chik-Chik!' Tufan slid off Makky's back and ran after the kipchali. All the animals had gone completely mad this morning! 'Come back! It's dangerous!' But Chik-Chik was not listening. Before Tufan could stop him, he and his friend began to slurp up water from the stream!

Half a ding to timeout and Puzzle Pod 3 nowhere in sight! Zvala took a bite of a Born-Again Bar and pedalled faster. Once again, the canal began to widen. Zvala fired the last few mashaalamps. By their flickering light, she saw ahead of her the dim outlines of a small island, and in the middle of it, a shadowy pyramid—the last puzzle pod!

Zvala pulled the boat up onto the island and ran towards the pyramid. Then she stopped short, teetering at the edge of a wide moat that encircled the pyramid. A fraying rope festooned with makdiboochi webs hung down from the ceiling. She tugged on the rope, checking if it would hold her weight. It seemed fine. She steeled herself. She could do this. She leaned over the edge of the moat to check how deep it was.

For a moment, Zvala did not understand what she was seeing. Then her eyes widened and her insides turned over in revulsion. Scurrying about in the darkness of the moat, their claws skittering on the stone floor, were hazillions and hazillions of creepy little thingachis! Zvala staggered away from the edge, feeling sick to her stomach.

After she had taken a long draught of water to settle herself, Zvala checked her dingdial. Twenty dinglings to go. It was now or never. She looked over the edge of the moat again and froze. She could not do this! Panic squeezed the breath from her lungs. What if the rope broke? What if she missed her footing on the other side? She would fall into the moat, and the thingachis would be all over her! Her skin crawled.

All of a sudden, something furry jumped onto her shoulder. Zvala screamed so loudly that she scared herself. The poor creature ran down her back and straight into her pocket, where it sat, cowering in fright. Pocket? There was something familiar about a furry thingachi in a pocket.

'Squik!' said Zvala softly. 'Is that you?' There was a small, nervous squeak. 'Oh, Squik! It *is* you!' laughed Zvala, her voice shaky. 'I never thought I'd actually be glad to see you.' She eased her fingers into her pocket

gently. The gileli climbed into her palm. Then it jumped off and raced to the edge of the moat, uttering a string of high-pitched squeaks.

One dingling ticked by, then another. The moat was eerily quiet. Gathering up her courage, Zvala leaned over the edge. The thingachis had rearranged themselves, leaving a clear path in between. If Zvala fell into the moat, she would certainly hurt herself, but she wouldn't have crawly things scrambling all over her. 'Thanks, Squik!' she said gratefully, holding out her palm. The gileli jumped in and headed straight for her pocket.

Zvala grabbed the rope and walked backwards as far as it would allow. Then she took a series of running steps, pulled herself up on the rope, and swung across the moat, jumping off safely on the other side. Twelve dinglings to go—Zarpa had said she should start thinking of leaving about now. But she had come too far, achieved too much already—she wasn't going to quit now. She hoped the last puzzle wasn't going to be too hard.

Zvala stepped into the dark pyramid and waited for instructions. With a deafening crash of cymbals, the lights came on. Zvala shaded her eyes—each wall of the pyramid was silvered and the lights were blinding. Whichever way she turned, she saw herself reflected—

a grimy, wet little mithyakin with straggly hair and terrified eyes.

'The I Pod!' snickered the genie, coming to life, a cloudy moving image as if made of smoke. CRACK! One of the mirrors broke into pieces and fell to the ground. Zvala stared—her reflection was still preserved in it, like a freezeframe! *'Rearrange the pieces quick, create again a picture slick, and be out of here in a tick.'*

A jigsaw puzzle! That was easy, especially when she herself was the subject! Zvala worked feverishly, cutting her fingers on the mirror shards. Done! The panel of the I Pod slid open. Zvala wiped her bleeding fingers on her lucky capris, grabbed the rope and swung herself across. Jumping into the boat, she began to pedal like one possessed.

Chik-Chik and the other kipchali stretched out on the grass, their heads cocked, basking in the heat of the arcalamps. Tufan watched them warily—would the water make them ill? Were their stripes going to turn into polka dots? Would they keel over and die? Nothing happened. Tufan began to relax. 'You worry needlessly, boy!' he said, rubbing Makky's neck affectionately.

Zarpa and Zub came racing around the side of Mankayos, looking worried. 'Has Zvala come out of the back gate, by any chance?' asked Zarpa. 'There are only five dinglings left for the game to time out.'

'No,' said Tufan, beginning to look anxious. 'Not here yet.'

'I hope she's . . .' began Zarpa, and then her mouth fell open. 'Wh-what are th-those?' she stuttered. Makky began to whimper again.

Tufan whirled around. On the grass by the inky stream, where Chik-Chik and his friend had been warming themselves just a dingling ago, stood two monster kipchalis! 'Whoaaa!' gasped Tufan. 'Just look at those . . .er . . . those . . . megakips!'

'Eeeeeeeeee!' A high-pitched squeal pierced the air. Now it was the megakips' turn to whimper.

Zarpa whooped. 'That's Zvala! But where *is* she?' She didn't have to wait long for an answer. The back gates of Mankayos burst open. Barrelling triumphantly down the stream in a batakoose-shaped pedal boat, her dirt-streaked face swathed in smiles, came the heroine of the octite, makdiboochi webs forming a halo around her happy head.

Twelve

Tufan stood alone on a desolate hilltop, completely lost, a thick fog swirling around him. Somewhere close was the Bel Nolo stadium, but the fog was so thick he could not see his own hand in front of his face. For a while, he had heard Zarpa and Zvala yelling for him and for each other, and he had yelled back until he was hoarse, but he hadn't heard anything now for almost a ding. They had almost certainly missed the deadline for their match.

Suddenly, from nearby, he heard the low growl of a shardula. Tufan froze. Another growl, this time from behind. The shardula was stalking its prey—him! There was nowhere to run! The mist cleared a little, revealing a filthy, inky stream flowing right by his feet. It looked vaguely familiar.

SNAAARL! A giant shardula leaped out of the stream, going straight for his face!

Tufan screamed and sat up in bed, drenched in sweat, breathing hard. Something *was* on his face, but it wasn't a shardula. 'Chik-Chik!' he scolded, once his heartbeat had returned to normal. 'What were you trying to . . .' He stopped short. 'Heyyyy! You're back to your old size! That's how you got in through the window! Uffpah— that's a relief—so the effects of that weird stream were not permanent . . .' The other kipchali stared up at him from the foot of the bed, blinking innocently.

'Tufan, are you okay?' Zarpa and Zvala were banging on his door. 'We heard you screaming . . .'

'I'm fine,' Tufan sounded sheepish. 'Bad dream. Go back to sleep.'

'Go back to sleep?' Zvala sounded incredulous. 'It's five o'ding, lazyboots—you've already overslept a couple of dings, and the Bel Nolo match starts at ten. Get out of there this instant!'

Tufan groaned. 'But do we know where to go yet?' he said, playing for time. 'No point in all of us sitting around waiting for instructions. Wake me up once you figure out the details . . .'

'Nice try!' laughed Zarpa. 'But this time there is no mystery—the match has been announced in this morning's *Sparkl Times*! It's happening at the Ring of Rann stadium, and all the Sparklkos are invited.'

'Unnngghhh!—see you in ten,' grumbled Tufan, diving under the bedclothes.

'Zub!' grinned Tufan, headbanging to the blast metal blaring out of the familiar blue-and-silver aquauto. 'Where did this come from?'

'Got it sent across from Lustr, express delivery!' grinned back Zub. 'For old times' sake!'

Zvala made a big show of groaning and shutting her ears. In reality, the sight of Zub's aquauto, which had ferried them to all their adventures in Lustr, had delighted her.

Zarpa felt better too. Titliflies had been fluttering around in her stomach ever since she had opened the morning newspapyrus, but now, watching Zub's braid swinging behind him as he drove, she felt a lot of the titliflies disappear. There was certainly a lot at stake today, but surely nothing that the Taranauts could not handle?

'Zub!' called Tufan. Zub turned down the music. 'Do you think you can get us there at least half a ding before the match begins? I'd like to meet the ashvequins we are going to ride, get to know them a little . . .'

'I'll try my best,' promised Zub.

'The Marani assured me she was going to organize the calmest and most sweet-tempered ashvequins for us,' smiled Zarpa.

'Uh-hunh,' Zvala's brow wrinkled with worry. 'But I have a feeling there will be a few surprises waiting for us.'

At the Ring of Rann stadium, a shadowy figure emerged around the corner of the Team Taranauts' stables, its upper half covered in a dark razuvet. Looking around stealthily to check that the coast was clear, it lifted the latch on the stable doors and pushed them open. It spoke softly to the three ashvequins inside, and led them gently out.

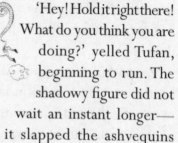

'Hey! Hold it right there! What do you think you are doing?' yelled Tufan, beginning to run. The shadowy figure did not wait an instant longer— it slapped the ashvequins hard on their rumps and scurried into the stadium, melting into the crowds. The animals galloped away into the woods, whinnying in alarm.

'Now what?' The Taranauts stood at the empty stables, furious.

There was a clatter of hooves behind them. 'Missing a few ashvequins, are we, mithyakins?' The jeer in Ograzur Dusht's voice was unmistakable. 'Tch, tch. Never mind, we'll think of some way to still make it a fair game.'

'Yeah, we *so* believe you, Mr. What's-his-name!' said Zvala.

'Dusht,' said Dusht, bending down and extending his hand. '*Ograzur* Dusht to you.'

'No, thanks,' snapped Tufan, folding his arms across his chest. 'Now, suppose you tell us how exactly we are supposed to play Bel Nolo without our ashvequins?'

'Oooh, the mithyakins have spirit!' Dusht pretended to shudder. 'I like it! Now, here's what we'll do—our team will not use ashvequins either. Instead, each team gets to pick any animal they like. If you are not ready by matchstart, though, you forfeit. Fair?'

'Extremely,' growled Zarpa.

'Harharazur!' chuckled Dusht. He pulled in the ashvequin's reins and rode off in a cloud of dust.

'Ten dinglings to match-start!' came the announcement over the volumizers. 'Downsiders versus . . . Taranauts!' At the sound of the last word, a huge cheer rose from the stadium. The familiar chanting began. 'Tara-NAUTS! Tara-NAUTS!'

'What shall we do?' wailed Zvala, beginning to turn red. 'What animals can we round up in just ten dinglings?'

'Even if Makky were here, he would only be one makara,' sighed Tufan.

'Oh, if only our kipchalis were still megakips . . .' sighed Zarpa.

'Oh! Oh! Oh! They *can* be!' cried Tufan. 'Zub made me fill a big bottle with that awful water—he said it might come in useful sometime.' He rummaged in his backsack. 'Here it is!'

'We still need another kipchali!' reminded Zvala.

'Let me find one for you,' said Zub, who had suddenly appeared by their side in his usual mystifying fashion.

He plunged into the woods behind the stables.

Tufan pulled Chik-Chik and the red-and-white kipchali away from the zamunberries in his pocket. Zarpa scoured the stables, returning quickly with a shallow bowl. 'Drink up, drink up quickly!' coaxed Tufan. The kipchalis slurped up the water happily.

'I see another kipchali!' yelled Zvala, as a flash of indigo appeared around the corner of the stables. 'Wait! I'll get him!'

Tufan and Zarpa exchanged disbelieving glances— well, well, there was something to be said for Mankayos, after all!

Zvala knelt on the ground, making soothing clicks with her tongue and using a bunch of zamunberries as bait. The kipchali devoured the berries, then slurped up the water from the bowl she held out to him.

'You guys start getting changed—I'll get the Bel Nolo sticks!' called Zarpa, running towards the team locker. Quickly, Zvala and Tufan pulled on their team jerseys and helmets, and took small bites of their Born-Again Bars.

'Testing . . . testing . . . check 1, 2, 3 . . .' Zvala spoke into the transmitter of her helmet Hummonica.

'Reading loud and clear,' said Tufan. Zarpa, who had just strapped on her helmet, nodded too.

'Should we feed the kipchalis some Born-Again Bars, do you think?' said Zarpa, handing out the sticks.

'I don't see why not,' replied Tufan, breaking off a piece

for Chik-Chik. 'They are going to need all the energy they can get.'

'Are we all set, Captain?' said Zvala.

'We are if *they* are,' replied Zarpa, turning to check. Then her thumb went straight up—the megakips were ready.

The Taranauts mounted their steeds awkwardly. 'Where did Zub go?' Tufan looked around anxiously. 'The poor guy must still be looking for a kipchali.'

'Oh, I wouldn't worry about Mr. Mysterious,' said Zvala darkly. She was very uncomfortable with Zub's habit of appearing and disappearing without explanation. 'Now, hurry up and tell us how to ride these guys!'

'Treat your megakip exactly like you would your ashvequin,' advised Tufan. 'Dig your heels into his sides if you want him to go faster, squeeze his left flank hard with your foot if you want to turn left, and the right flank if you want to turn right. Kipchalis can be very swift—at least when they are normal-sized—so hold on tight.'

'Huddle!' called Zarpa. The Taranauts slid off their megakips and hunched in a circle, their arms around each other. '*Who's the team with the big, big dream? We a-a-are, we are!*' they chanted. '*We'll crack each clue, till we rescue, each glo-o-owing star! Go-ohhhh, Taranauts!*'

They rode into the cheering stadium, the same thought sending a little icy trickle down their spines—what terrible animal would the Downsiders be riding?

Thirteen

Zarpa scanned the circular Bel Nolo field. Everything seemed to be in order. In the middle of the field was the stack of eight coloured discs that both teams would be trying to smack into one of the eight 'pockets' around the edge of the field. The discs had been placed, as usual, in the order in which they had to be pocketed, with the lowest value disc on top. She ran her eyes down the stack, mentally going over their values. Violet carried one point, so did indigo. Under indigo was blue—2 points, then green—3, yellow—5, orange—8, red—13, and white—21. And . . . black?

Zarpa stared. What was a black disc doing in Bel Nolo? That made it nine discs! 'Team,' she spoke into her helmet transmitter. 'Something's funny—see the black disc at the bottom of the stack?'

'Hmm,' replied Tufan. 'Don't let's worry about it too much right now, though—we will figure it out by and by.'

'Yes,' agreed Zvala, her voice uneven. 'We have other things to worry about right now. Look who's coming in—and on what!'

With a great shout of 'Harharazur!', the rival team thundered into the stadium, faint amethyst Taralite glinting off their polished helmets, Bel Nolo sticks raised high above their heads. They rode ferocious wilderwolves that snarled and spat, their long yellow fangs dripping drool, their sinewy bodies rippling under thick silver fur. A hush fell over the stadium. There was no way the three scared-looking mithyakins on those weird reptiles could beat the Downsiders!

'Tufan, mark the player in the No. 11 jersey!' ordered Captain Zarpa, struggling to stay focused on the game. 'Zvala, stick to No. 17 like a khoonsucker. I'll shadow No. 10.' Tufan crooned soothingly to the terrified megakips, trying to calm them down.

'Welcome to Ring of Rann!' boomed a familiar voice over the volumizers. 'This octite's tie—Downsiders versus Taranauts!' The Taranauts recoiled as Ograzur Dusht strode into the centre of the field on an ashvequin, wearing a jersey with the words 'REFEREE' emblazoned on it. Their hearts sank—now their chances of winning this match were next to nil.

'I demand a change of referee!' a second voice, also familiar, said firmly over the volumizers. 'In fact, I *command* it!' A great cheer went up in the stadium. The Taranauts raised their sticks gratefully to the VIM (Very Important Mithyakos) box to their right—hurray for the Marani of Sparkl!

Dusht cast a look of pure venom in the Taranauts' direction. Then, with almost the entire stadium booing him, he galloped off, heartily cursing Ograzur Vak. It had been the old mithyaka who had insisted on a public match, arguing that it would get the Downsiders good publicity for their cause. If Shaap Azur had listened to him, Dusht, instead, the match would have been quietly played on a remote field with no witnesses and with him as referee, and the brats would already have been on their way home now, defeated. He ground his teeth in frustration—one dastardly plan had failed, but no matter, he had others up his sleeve.

The referee's whistle blew. Both teams raced to the centre of the field, sticks at the ready. No. 11 got there first and swung powerfully at the stack. The discs flew into the air, scattering across the field.

'The violet's mine!' Tufan called, digging his heels into Chik-Chik's sides and chasing after No. 11. Out of the corner of her eye, Zvala saw No. 17 swing his stick—he was going to distract Tufan by sending the red disc at him!

Quickly, she raced into position. When the red disc flew into the air, she blocked it with her stick, tossed it high into the air and smacked it across the field as it fell.

'Pocketed!' screamed Tufan from somewhere behind her. A roar went up from the crowd. One point to the Taranauts!

The chase began again. The discs flew into the air in every direction, making it difficult for both teams to keep their eyes on the indigo. The referee raced around the players, his ashvequin keeping pace steadily with the megakips and wilderwolves. No. 11 raised his stick triumphantly. The whistle went. The indigo had been pocketed—one point to the Downsiders.

'Eyes peeled, team! Go for the blue!' yelled Zarpa. A dingling later, four discs whined through the air at her—surely one of them was blue? She swung wildly to defend herself—and connected. A light-coloured disc spun through the air and landed within the safe zone of the eastern pocket—blue! Tweet!

The referee pointed at Zarpa—the shot was hers to take. She sped to the safe zone, then brought her stick down and turned it so that its flat circular face was level with the motionless disc. 'Full focus!' said Tufan. Zarpa swung the stick slowly back and forth a few times, her eye firmly on the line between disc and pocket. She swung the stick one final time and struck the disc firmly. The disc skimmed the ground, heading straight for the pocket, and dropped into it. Two more points to the Taranauts!

Once again, the discs flew as the teams raced around the field. 'I'll take the green,' called Zvala, beginning to chase it single-mindedly. No. 17 kept pace grimly at her side, determined to pocket the three-pointer before she did. Zarpa and Tufan played their parts competently, keeping No. 11 and No. 10 at a safe distance from Zvala.

The green disc was just ahead of her. Zvala dug her heels into her megakip's side, urging it to put on an extra burst of speed. The green disc was now within striking range. Zvala raised her stick, aimed, and swung. The next instant, she had tumbled off her megakip and was rolling on the ground, right in the path of the steely claws of No. 17's wilderwolf! The last thing she saw before she blacked out was her limping, whimpering megakip, a gaping hole where its left foreleg used to be!

'Zvala! Are you okay?' Zvala opened her eyes. Her friends' blurry faces were bent worriedly over her. 'I'm fine!' she said weakly. 'What just happened?'

'The bad news first,' Tufan said hurriedly. 'So No. 17 pocketed the green, and his wilderwolf bit off your megakip's leg.' Zvala blanched, looking ready to pass out again. 'The good news,' Tufan went on hurriedly, 'is that kipchalis have the power to grow back any limb they lose, and with a little help from Twon d'Ung's Born-Again Bars, your megakip is now as good as new.'

'Yay!' Zvala got to her feet, fuming. 'Now let's give the crooked Downsiders all we've got!'

A deafening cheer went up from the stadium at Zvala's quick recovery. She mounted her megakip, making soothing clicks with her tongue. The referee blew his whistle. The chase resumed.

But Zvala's megakip had completely lost its spirit. Chik-Chik also looked traumatized, cowering and whimpering pitifully every time a wilderwolf came close. Astoundingly, Zarpa's indigo-striped megakip seemed to be immune to wilderwolf terror—it zipped in and out from between the wolves' feet like a seaslith, confusing the beasts completely.

Even the fastest megakip, however, could not be in three places at the same time. 'Yellow's gone too!' wailed Zvala, as the Downsiders' score zoomed. Downsiders—9, Taranauts—3.

Zarpa tore after the orange disc as it headed towards the safe zone, determined to win the eight-pointer. As she bore down on it, getting ready to strike, No. 17 bent smoothly from his wilderwolf and stretched out his stick-holding arm straight into their path! The megakip tripped and stumbled, throwing her off.

'FOUL!' screamed the crowd. The referee blew his whistle. 'Penalty stroke!' he called, pointing to Zarpa.

'Yay!' yelled Zvala and Tufan. 'Go for it, Captain!' The orange disc lay on the ground in the safe zone. Zarpa aimed carefully, and struck. The disc slid straight into the pocket! Downsiders—9, Taranauts—11!

But the very next dingling, the tables had turned again—No. 11 whooped as he pocketed the red! Zarpa's megakip raced towards the white disc, but it was gone in a flash, claimed by No. 10. Downsiders—43, Taranauts—11. Now there was only one disc left—black.

The volumizers around the field burst into life. 'If it pleases the referee,' Dusht's voice was exaggeratedly polite, 'the Downsiders would like to request a two-dingling timeout.' The referee nodded, signalling a timeout.

Dusht rode out into the centre of the field. 'The poor, poor mithyakins,' he cooed. '*Such* an unequal contest.' Still, my Master has one last challenge for you—your fourth riddle. Crack it—and you can play for the black. Don't, and you're out of the game.'

The Taranauts sat up, fully alert. All was not lost!

'You see the black disc?' he said, pointing. 'We added it many octons ago to our version of Bel Nolo. Now, how many points would you stand to win if you pocketed it? Guess! You only have until the end of timeout!'

Zarpa looked at her teammates blankly. How in Kay Laas were they to guess the value of the black disc? She called them into a quick huddle.

'The values of the other discs are completely random, aren't they, apart from the fact that they are in ascending order?' said Tufan. 'So there's no way to *calculate* the value of the next one.'

'Are you sure there isn't a pattern?' asked Zvala, wishing she had a scratchscribe handy. '1, 1, 2, 3, 5, 8, 13, 21. There must be *some* pattern . . .' She closed her eyes, focusing on the numbers in her head. 'Why are there two 1's?' wondered Zarpa. 'No other number is repeated.'

Tufan frowned. 'Okay, suppose we leave out one of the 1's. Then, there is no number between 1 and 2, no number

between 2 and 3, two numbers between 3 and 5, three numbers between 5 and 8 . . . hey, that's a pattern!'

'Doesn't work for 8 and 13, does it?' said Zvala. 'According to your pattern, there should be four numbers in between them, but there are five . . .'

She stared at the numbers again. 'Sometimes, it helps to add a 0 at the beginning of a list of numbers to see a pattern,' she said doubtfully. 'If we did that here . . . ' She 'saw' the list in her mind again. 'Let's see—0 plus 1 is 1, 1 plus 1 is 2, 1 plus 2 is 3, 3 plus 2 is 5 . . .' Her voice rose with excitement. 'That's it!' she cried. 'Each number in our new list is the sum of the two previous numbers! So the value of the black disc is 13 plus 21. . .'

'34!' announced Zarpa, just as the referee signalled the end of the timeout.

Dusht's oily smile vanished. 'Which means,' Zvala looked straight into his mean eyes, 'that if we pocket the black disc, *we can still win*!'

Dusht's face blazed with anger. 'Finish the brats, Downsiders!' he barked. 'Harharazur!'

Swinging his stick viciously, No. 17 put the black disc into play. Zarpa's megakip zipped after it on winged feet. Zvala and Tufan circled the field at a safe distance from the wilderwolves, passing the disc unerringly to Zarpa each time it sailed close to them.

Whooosh! The black disc whistled past Zarpa's ear and sped ahead of her. 'Let's get this, Kip!' she yelled. As she chased the disc, the Downsiders whirled and rode away in different directions. Then they turned and began to thunder down the field towards Zarpa, their wilderwolves snarling menacingly as they made straight for her megakip!

Zarpa's blood froze in her veins. If she had any sense at all, she should escape, now, to save herself and her megakip. But the disc was almost within striking range, and a pocket loomed close. She *had* to see this through!

An instant before the wilderwolves pounced, Zarpa struck. The disc sped straight to the pocket and tumbled in.

The crowd went insane. Zarpa raised her Bel Nolo stick in triumph, then stopped, her mouth falling open. She was standing on the ground. Around her, the three wilderwolves had stopped in mid-lunge, looking equally baffled. Her megakip had disappeared into thin air!

Fourteen

Emperaza Shoon Ya turned off the arcalamps in the tower room of his palace and stood still for a dingling, revelling in the amethyst light pouring in from the east. He shook his head in admiration—incredibly, the three mithyakins had succeeded yet again—but a twinge of real guilt followed immediately. With each rescue, he mused, Shaap Azur was getting more anxious, and a desperate foe could be very dangerous to his young heroes.

'The Achmentors are here, Emperaza,' Shuk Tee swept into the room.

Shoon Ya turned to face them, smiling. 'Your wards have outdone themselves, Achmentors—congratulations!' he said warmly. 'They are wonderful testimonials to your skills as teachers.'

The Achmentors bowed. 'We only do our duty, Emperaza Shoon Ya.'

Shoon Ya nodded. Then his eyes lit up, as if a splendid idea had suddenly occurred to him. 'I shall convene a new top-notch advisory council to the Emperaza. If the three of you would do me the honour of sitting in, I would be grateful.'

'Of course, Emperaza. It would be our privilege.' Bowing again, the Achmentors left the room.

'Emperaza, do you realize what you have just done?' burst out Shuk Tee, her forehead creasing in annoyance, the moment the door had shut behind them.

'What have I done?' Shoon Ya looked genuinely puzzled.

'These are bad times, Emperaza. We don't know where the mithyakos' loyalties lie. You do realize that Shaap Azur could not have escaped so easily from the Fiery Lands unless there were people from our side secretly supporting him.' Her voice rose steadily. 'And here you are, recruiting the Achmentors—who, by the way, are as suspect as anyone else—into your "top-notch advisory council", without even *discussing* it with me beforehand . . .'

'The Emperaza has every right to keep his own counsel,' Shoon Ya said, his voice steady. 'He is not bound to discuss anything,' he paused significantly, 'with *anyone*!'

Shuk Tee looked taken aback. 'Pardon me,' she snapped. 'But this is not about you—this is about Mithya.'

'Between me, the Achmentors, and the Taranauts,' retorted Shoon Ya. 'Mithya is already in fine hands, thank you.'

Anger and hurt blazed in Shuk Tee's eyes. She turned on her heel and left the room. ShoonYa was instantly sorry. He made to call out after her, then caught himself. Even the Most Intelligent Being in Mithya did not get away with speaking to the Emperaza that way.

'What do you do with gifted mithyakins who will simply not use their gifts?' Zub shook his head incredulously. 'For instance, how come you, Ms Zarpa, never thought of using your superstretch to get to the Bel Nolo discs ahead of the Downsiders—ever?'

'Oh, I could have done that, couldn't I?' said Zarpa, her eyes round. 'What a sillykoof I am!'

Everyone burst out laughing. It was a happy group at breakfast this morning—Zvala and Tufan on either side of Zub, Zarpa happily sandwiched between her parents, and at the head of the table, the Marani of Sparkl herself. In the evening, the Taranauts would be feted at a glittering public ceremony at the Ring of Rann, but just now, they were glad to be sitting out in the garden in the cool purple light of the Amethysts.

'And how come,' said Zvala, looking sharply at Zub, 'you took so long to look for a little kipchali?'

'Hey,' shrugged Zub, 'not my fault if the only one in the entire wood decides to jump into your palm! But I did return in time to watch the entire match.'

Zvala shook her finger at him, far from convinced. The others didn't seem to notice it, but she always felt there was something a little off about Zub.

'And how come,' demanded Tufan, 'there are no more pots of chilled creamy kulfice on this table?' He proceeded to lick his empty pot clean with his tongue.

'Ewww! Gross!' said Zvala, reaching behind Zub's back to bop Tufan's head.

'Timeout!' laughed the Marani. 'Now listen up. You mithyakins will receive your special medals this evening, but here are a few small gifts for you from me.' She clapped her hands. Three attendants appeared, staggering under the weight of gaily gift-wrapped boxes. The Taranauts whooped.

'Don't tear off the paper, you guys!' said Zvala, running to her boxes. 'I want to save the wrappers—they are soooooo beautiful!'

'Bet I got the most mastastic stuff of all!' Zarpa turned cartwheels on the grass. 'Black and silver all-terrain Obverse Nanos that convert to rollerblades and skis and whatnot, an all-weather durdekscope that helps you zoom in on stuff upto ten milyards away, and a latlongometer—I can never get lost again!' She ran to the Marani and threw her arms around her.

'Glolight gels in eight different colours!' squealed Zvala. 'And a monogrammed lavender backsack! And my own pocket wikipad! AND a pair of lavender all-terrain Nanos with gold swirls. Thank you so, so very much!'

Tufan's face filled with wonder as he checked out his goodies. He could not remember when he had last received a gift. 'All-terrain Nanos with blast guitarele designs!' he whispered. 'My own crittercaller, with the call of every animal and hakibyrd on Mithya preprogrammed! And all kinds of killer gizmotronic stuff! You totally rock, your Starness!'

Zvala and Zarpa ran to him as he bent down to open his last gift. It was wrapped in a double-layered scentlock bag and its shape looked suspiciously like a giant can of . . . 'Max alert!' yelled Zarpa. 'Oh no, you don't!' shouted Zvala. The three of them rolled round and round in the grass, wrestling with a whopper can of Triple Power Max.

In the Land of Nevernite, the palace of the Emperaza slept, slatblinds drawn against the light of the twelve rescued Tarasuns. In the quiet, a tall, slim figure stole lightly up the stairs to the tower room and entered as softly as a shadow.

When she had made sure she was alone, Shuk Tee sat cross-legged on the floor, exactly at the centre of the circle. She closed her eyes and slowly wound her body down to a state of absolute stillness. Stellipathic thoughtwaves radiated from her and travelled outwards like ripples in a pool to the far ends of Mithya, seeking other thoughtwaves, particularly those issuing from the Downsides. If the Emperaza would not listen to her, she would have to hunt down the enemies of Mithya on her own.

A mazillion thoughtwaves assaulted her instantly. So many mithyakos, so many thoughts! The trick was to sort rapidly through the raucous babble to the thoughts that were relevant. The challenge was trying to hack into the thoughts of the important Downsiders, who were all trained, like her, to keep their thoughtwaves locked in.

'*Those bratty Taranauts are finished . . .*' Shuk Tee tensed, concentrating. '*. . . breakthrough at last . . .*' The thoughtwave began to break up and get garbled—the thinker was locking in! Shuk Tee focused harder, breaking out into a sweat. '*It's a VIM . . . access to classified information . . . has defected . . . the Master will be pleased . . .*' The thoughtwave went silent.

Shuk Tee opened her eyes, her face grim. Her worst nightmare had come true. Someone high up in the Emperaza's administration—a Very Important Mithyaka—had turned traitor!